Please sign here:

_____

Here: _____

And here: _____

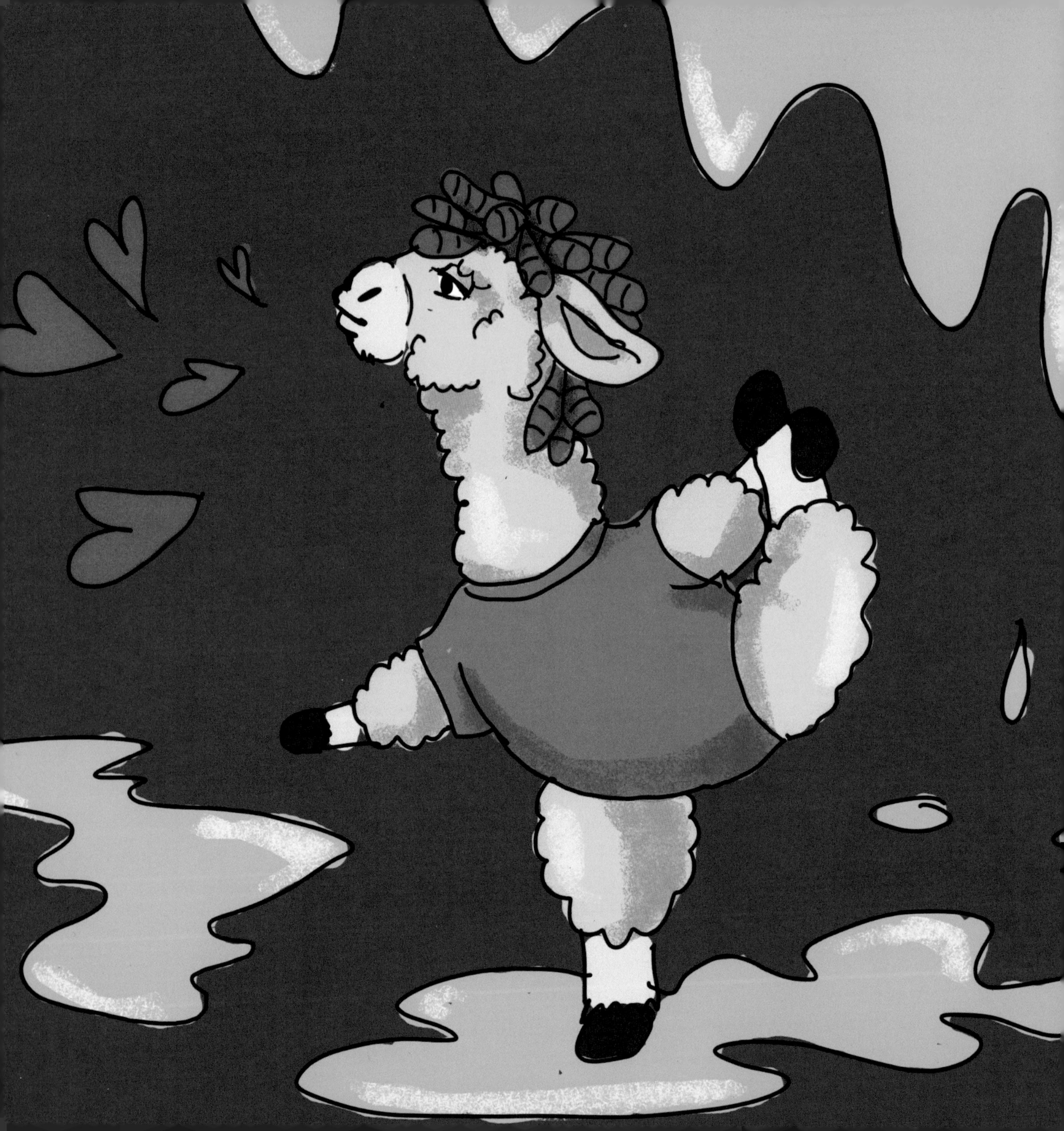

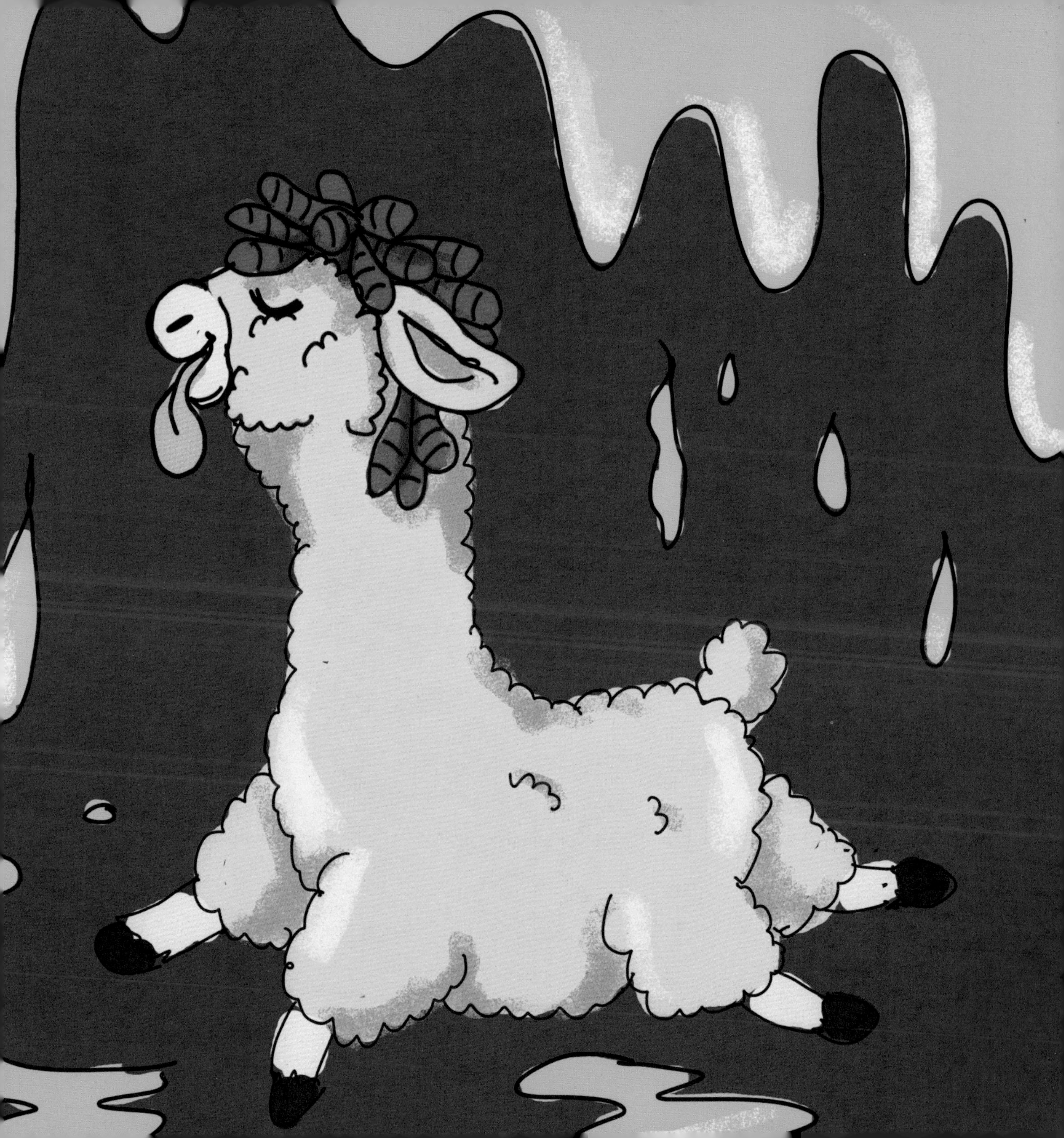

Never EVER Lick a Llama

By Adam Wallace
and Mary Nhin

Pictures by
Jelena Stupar

Printed and bound in the USA. 978-1-63731-081-6
Visit us at NeverEverBooks.com

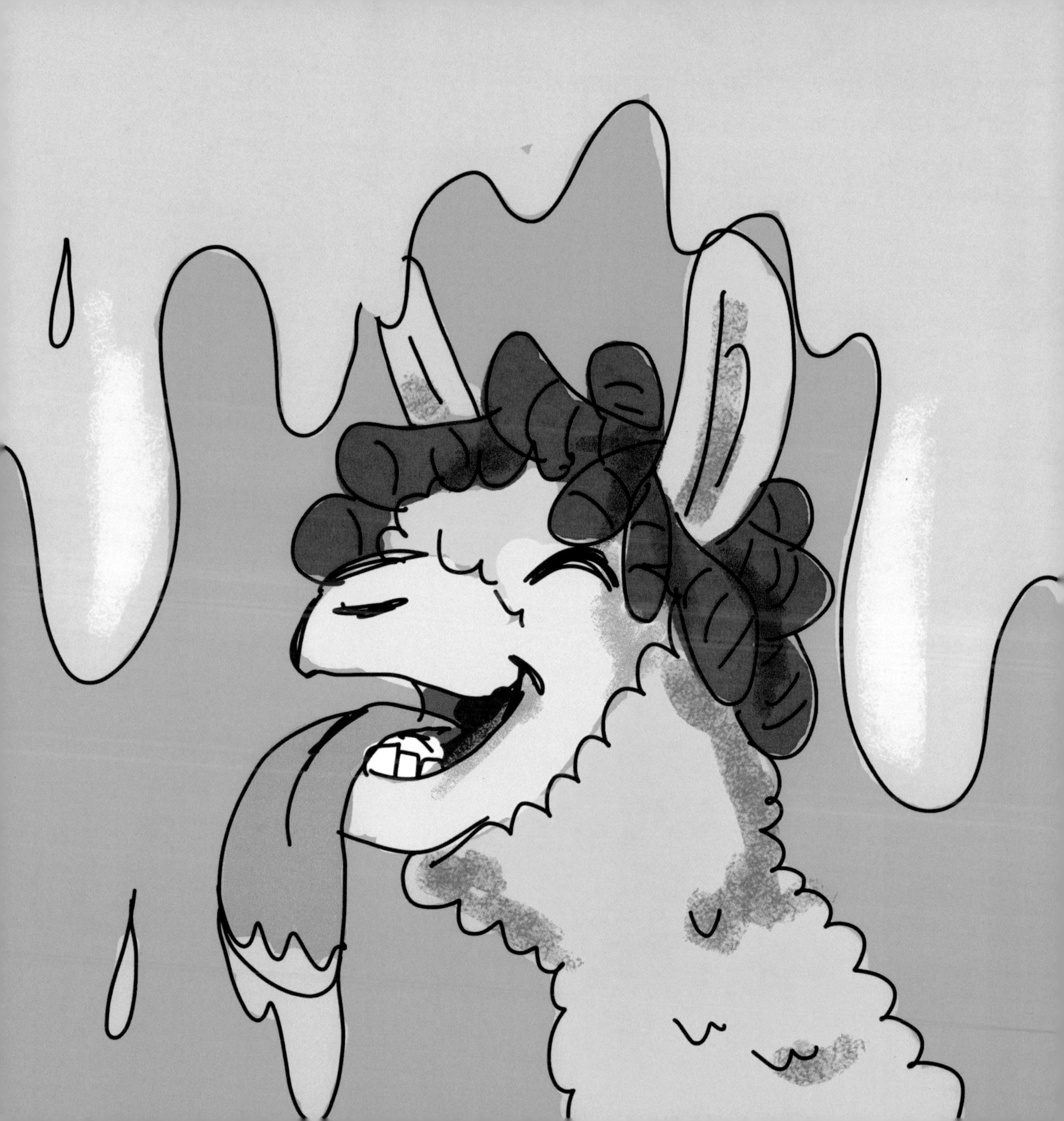

EVERYBODY loves llamas,
We know that much is true.
But if you want that love to last,
There's one thing you must do.

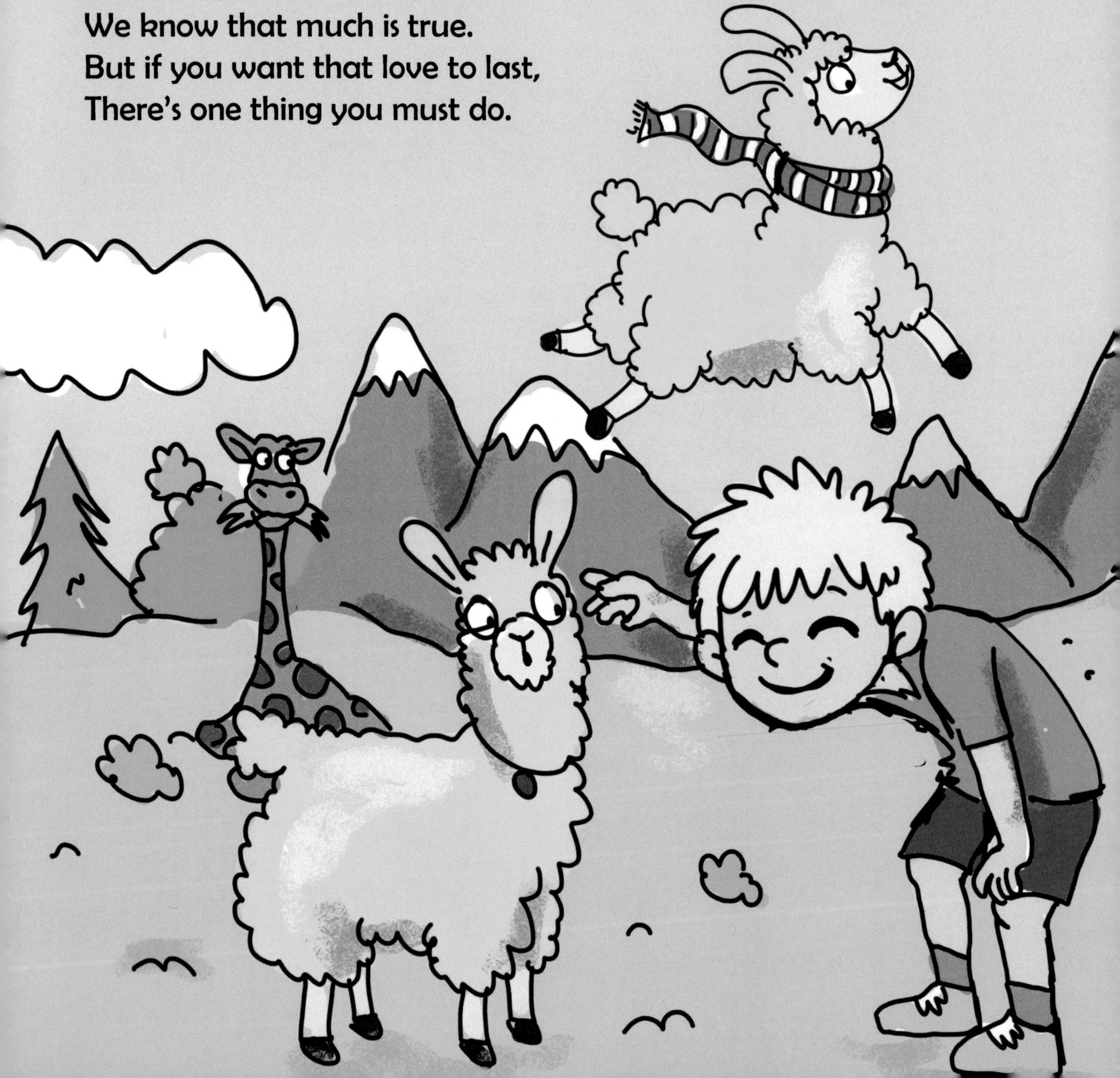

And that thing is ...

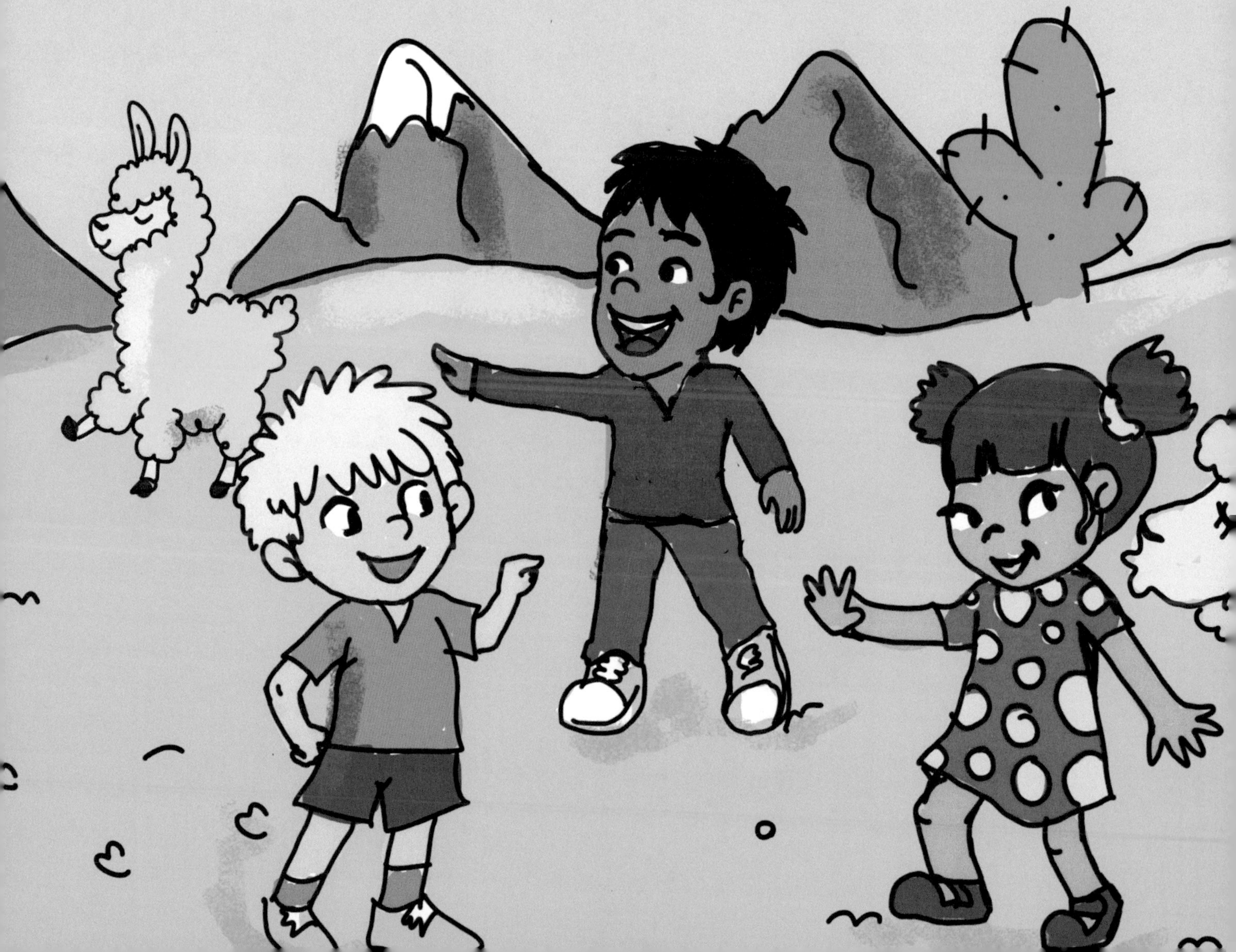

Never **EVER** lick a llama.
Why? The reasons are immense.
Decide **NOW** not to do it,
Don't sit on the fence.

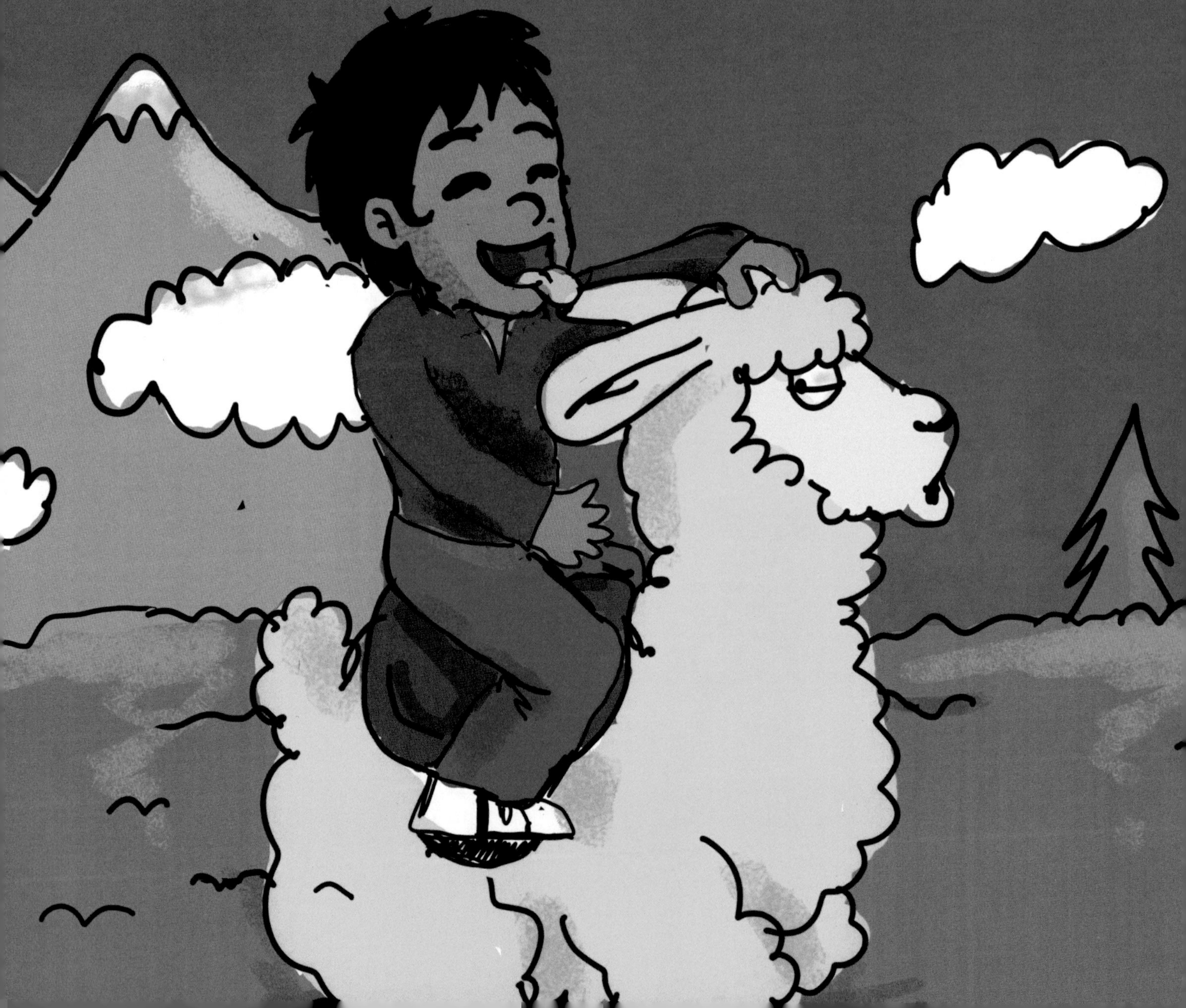

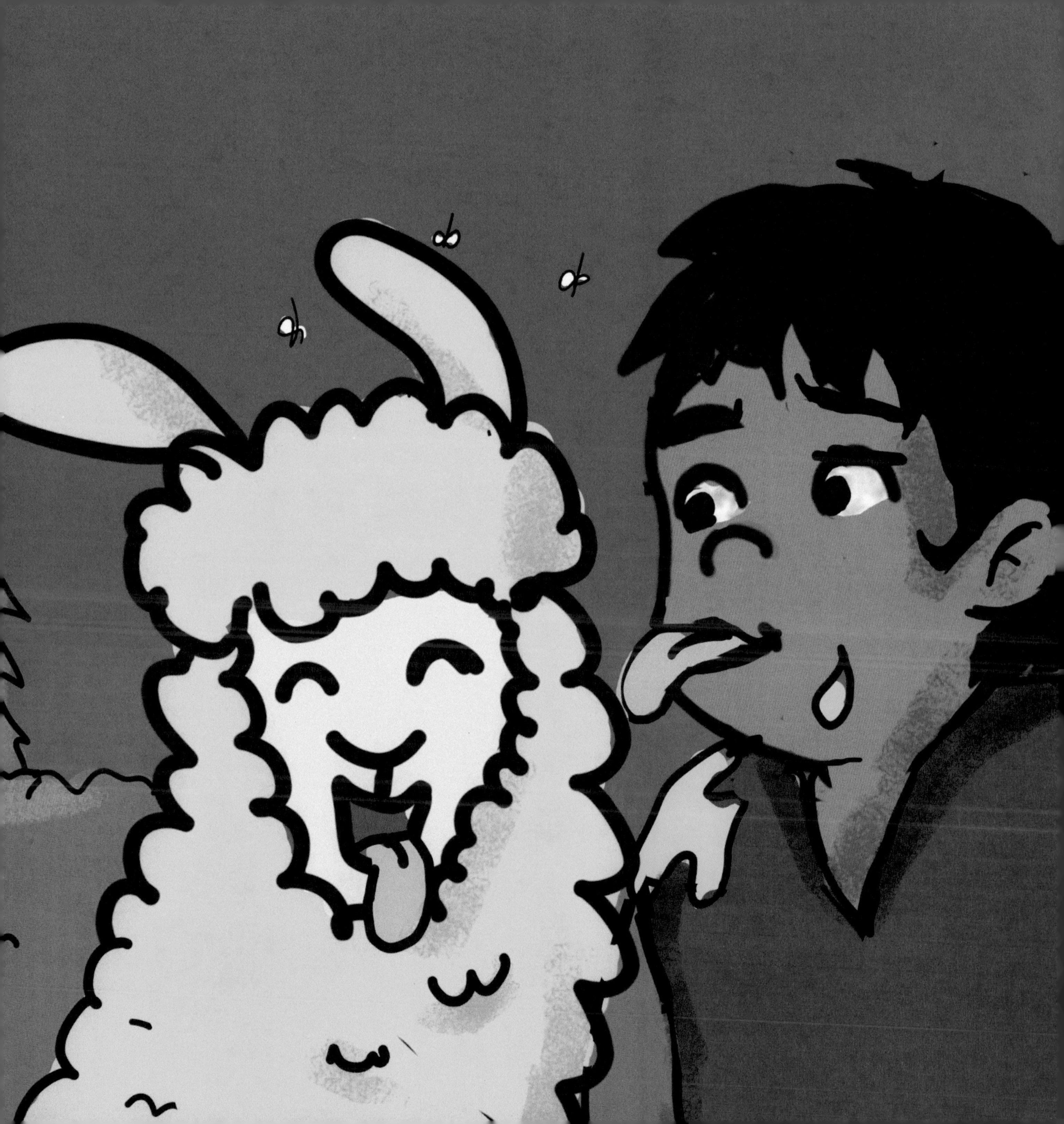

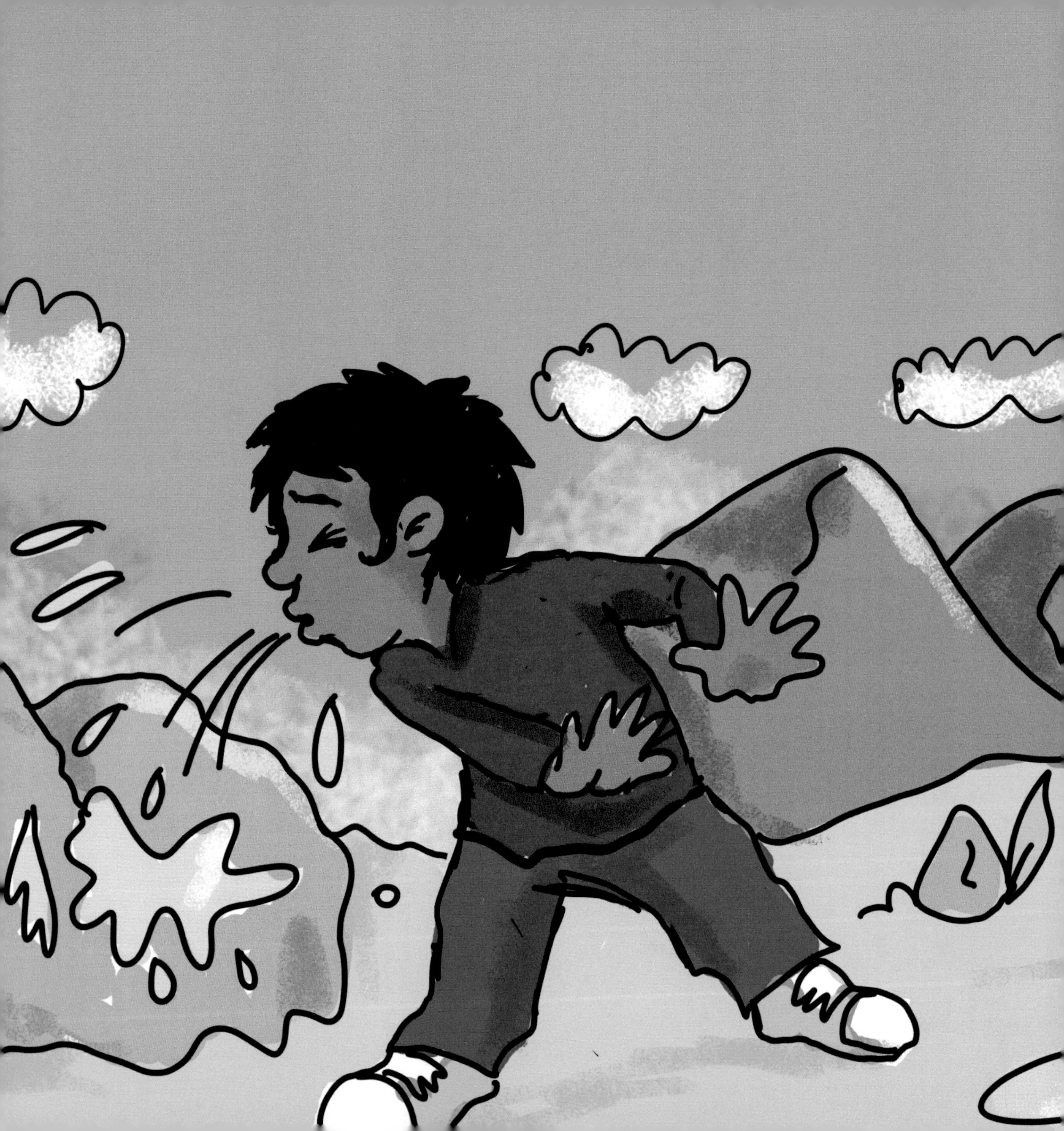

For starters, they're all fuzzy.
Why put your tongue on that?
Licking fur's a bad idea
Unless you are a cat.

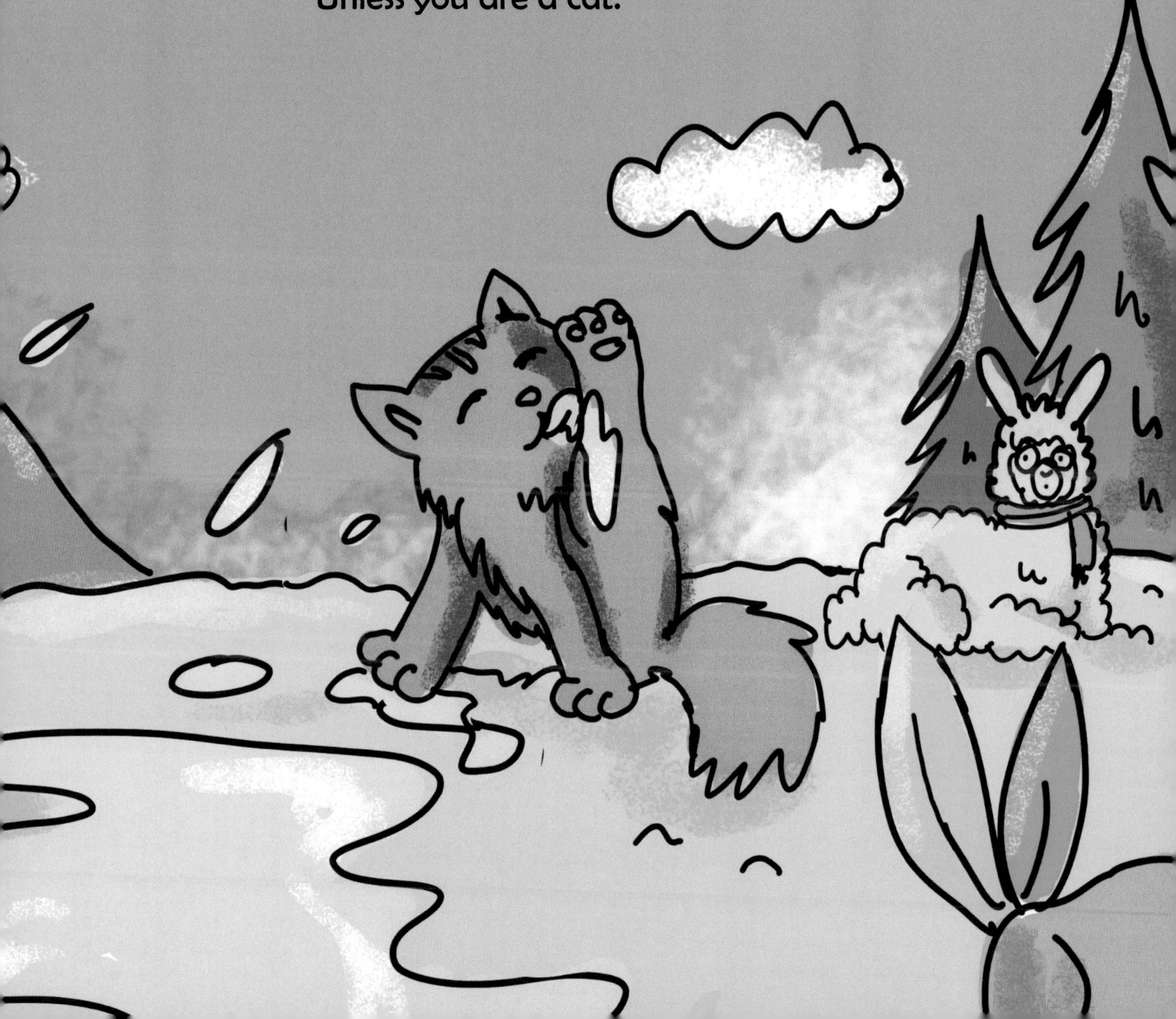

Should you lick it on the face?
Perhaps. There's much less fuzz.
No. It'll lick your face right back.
That's what a llama does!

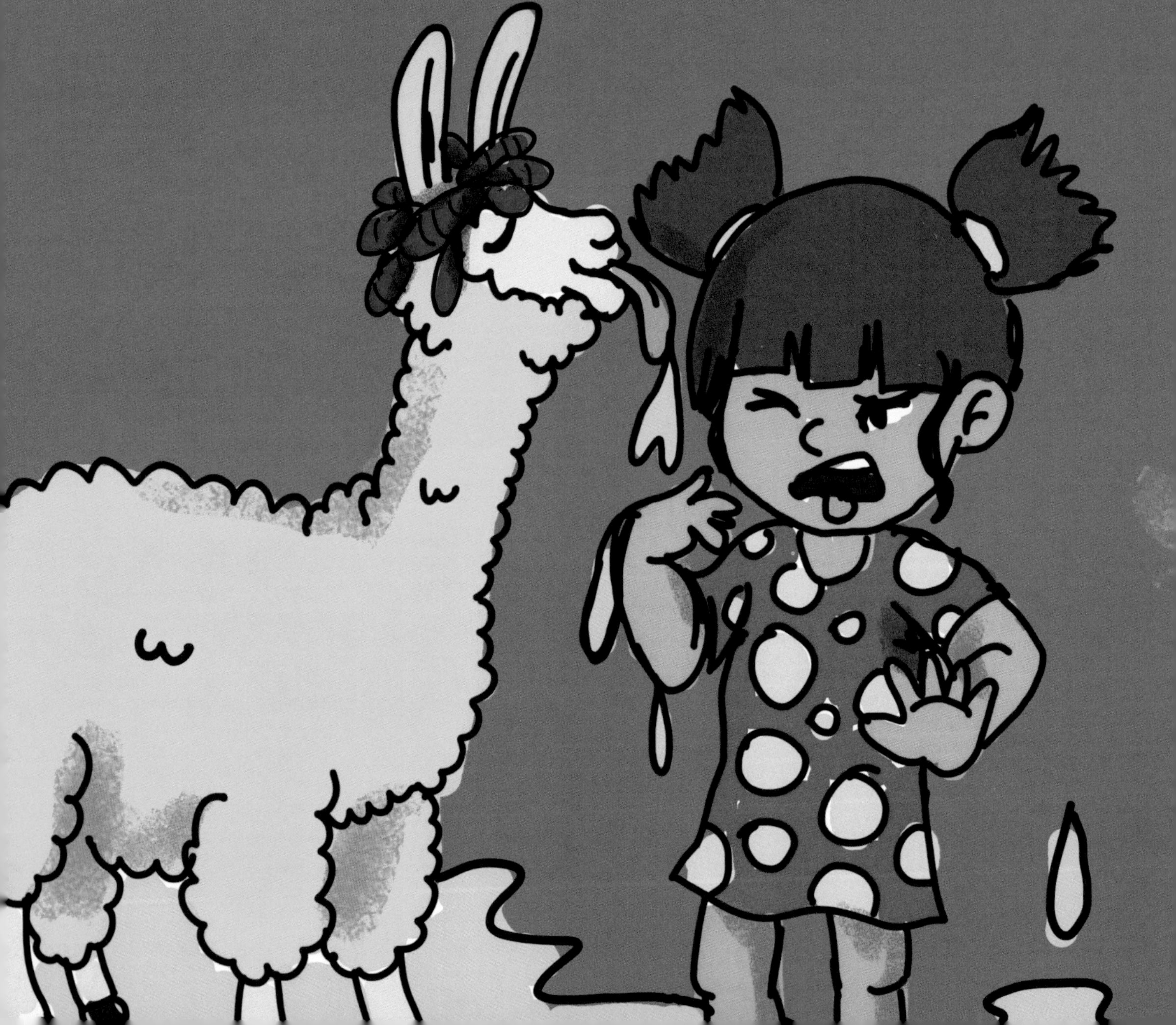

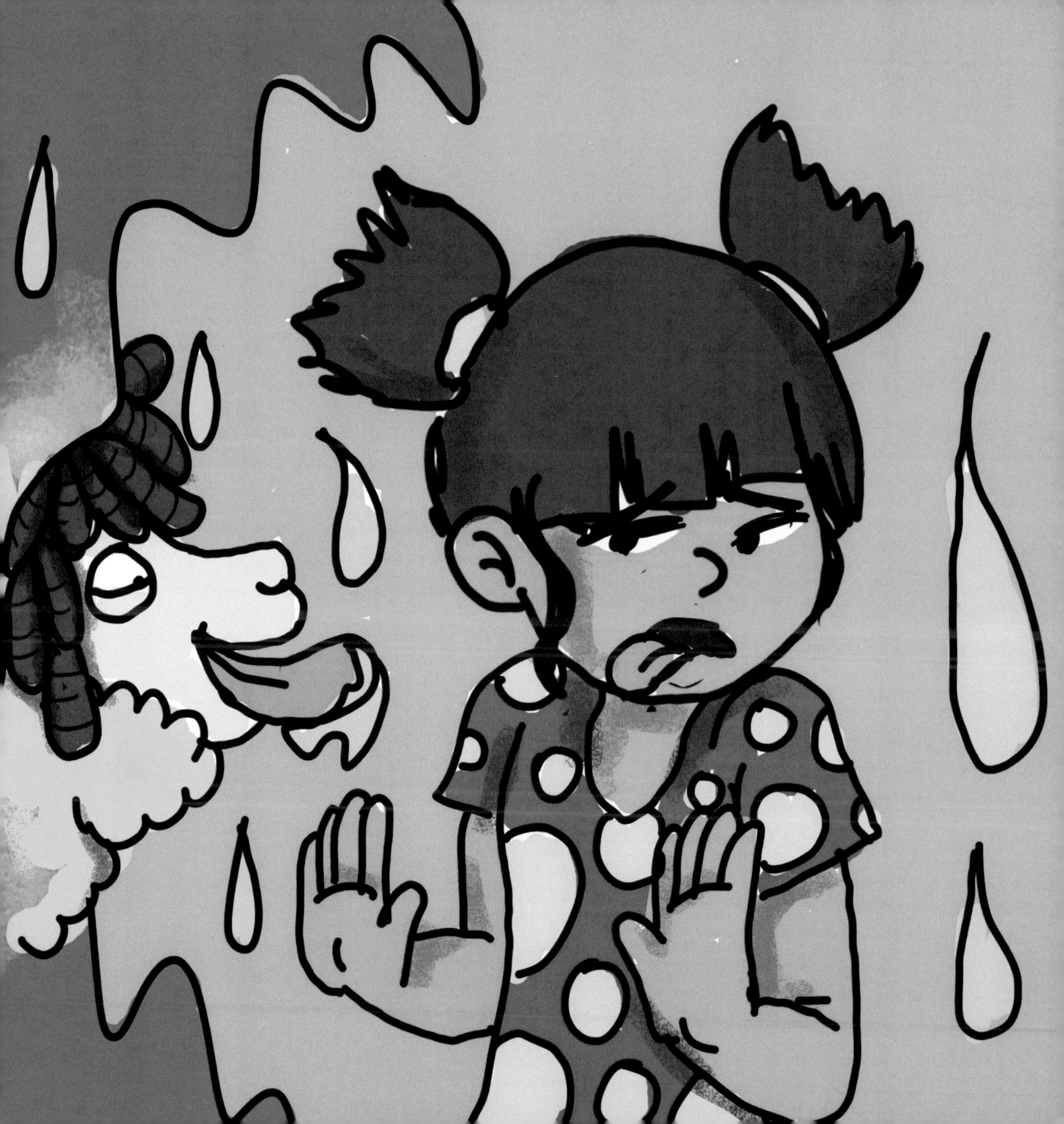

And if you are unlucky,
And lick at the same time,
Then you will lick a llama's tongue.
That's **NEVER EVER** fine!

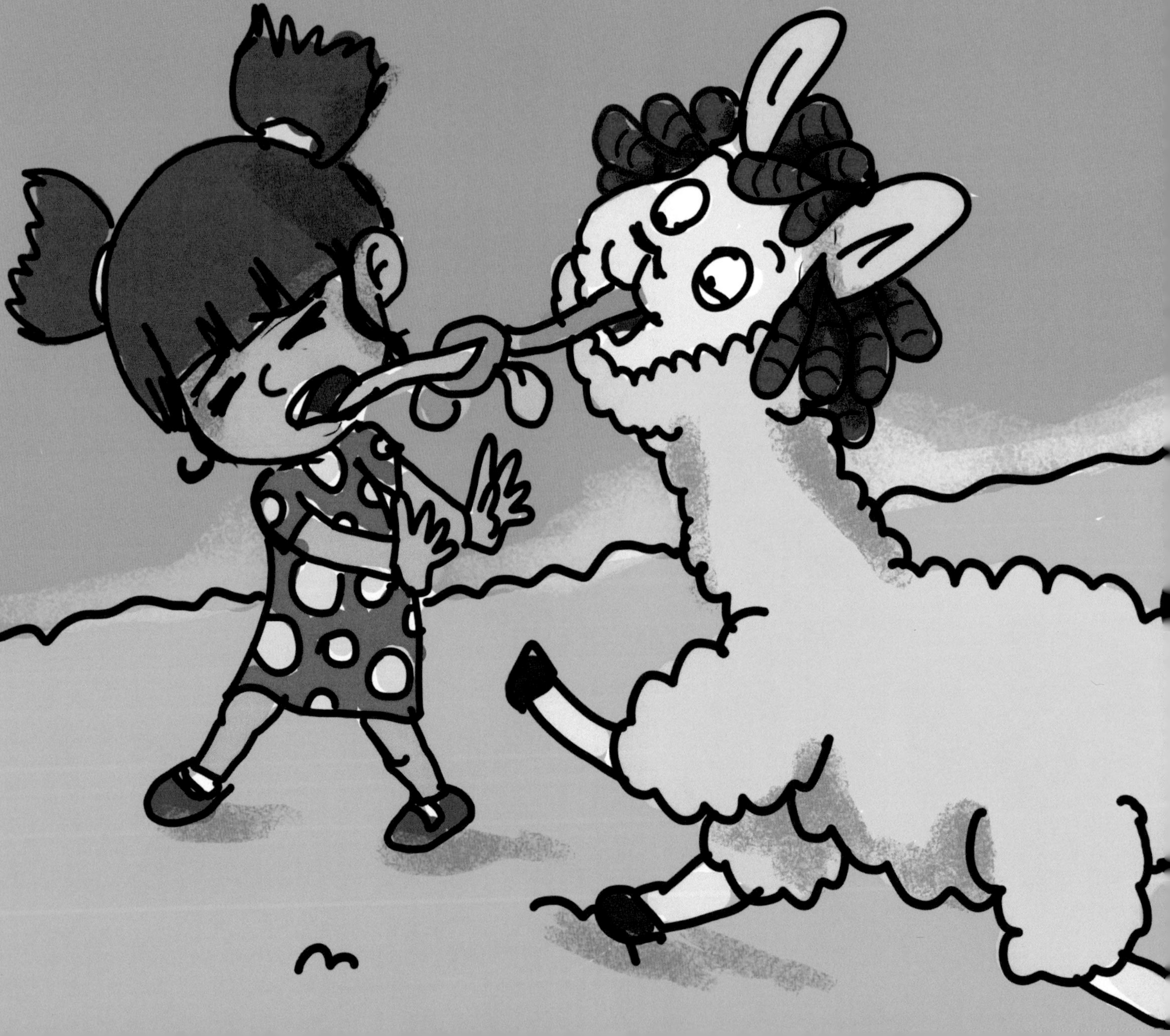

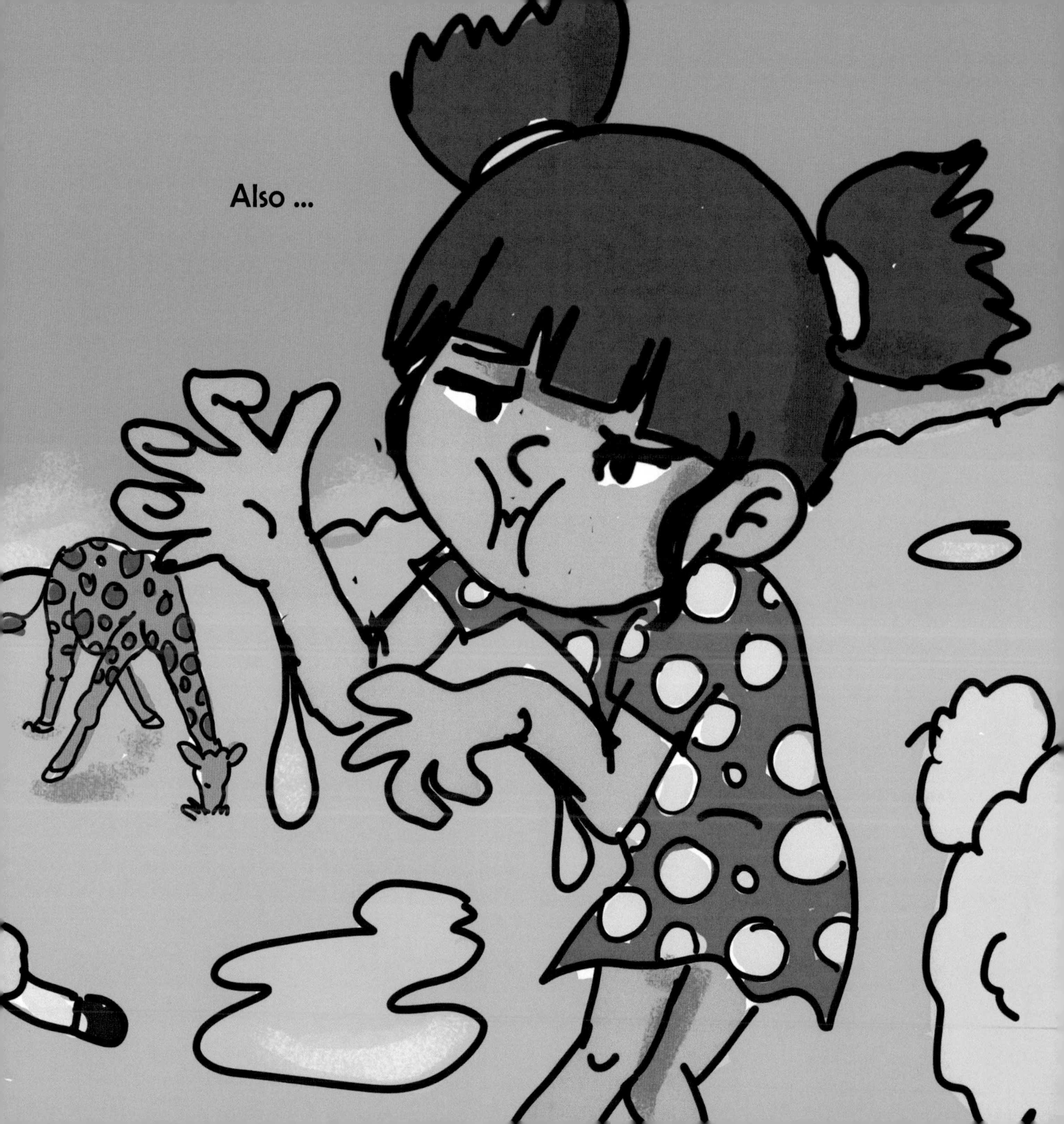
Also ...

Never **EVER** lick a lion.
That's just common sense.
And just like with a llama,
The reasons are immense.

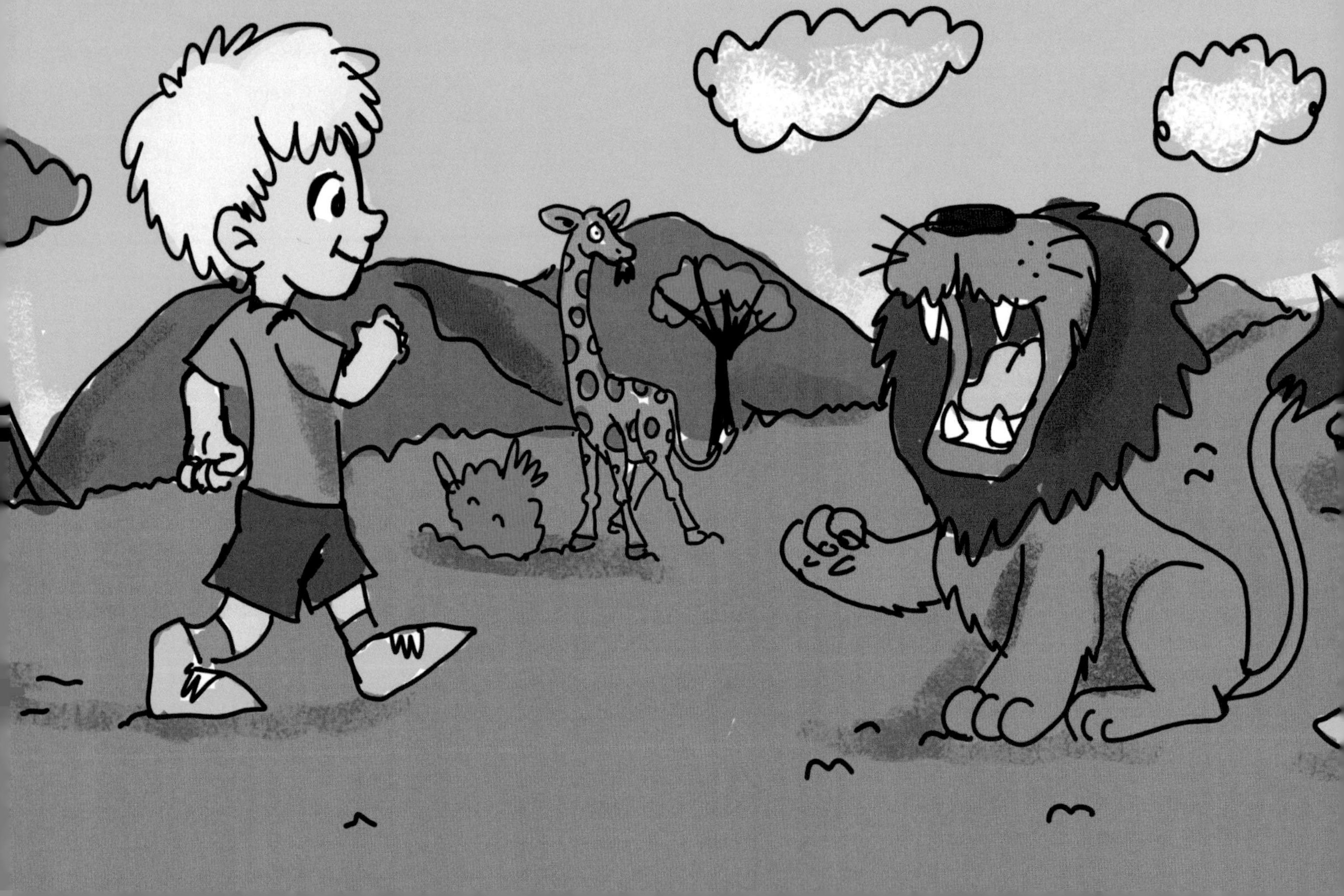

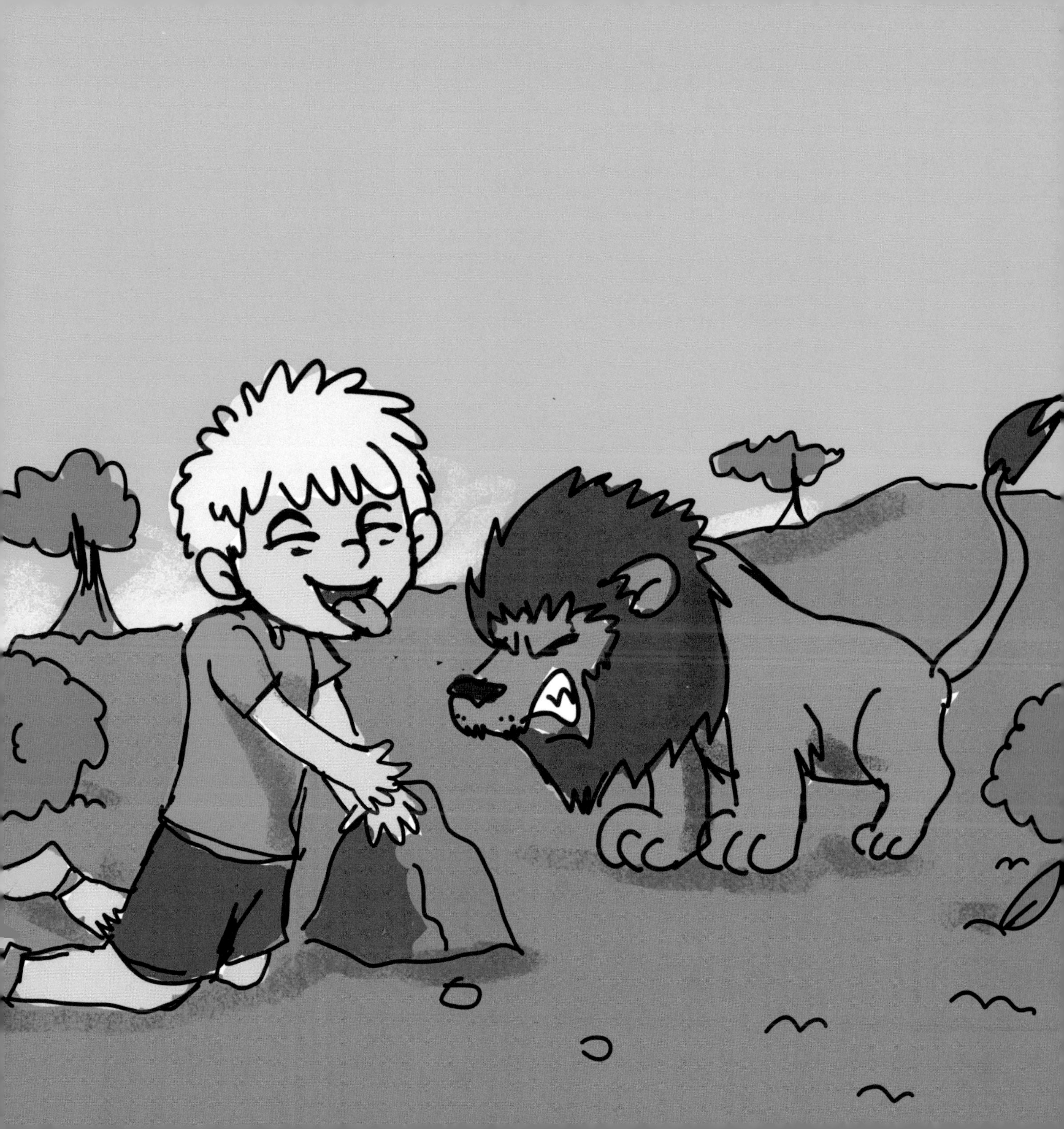

For starters ... **IT'S A LION!**
That's reason number one.
Here is reason number two ...
SEE REASON NUMBER ONE!

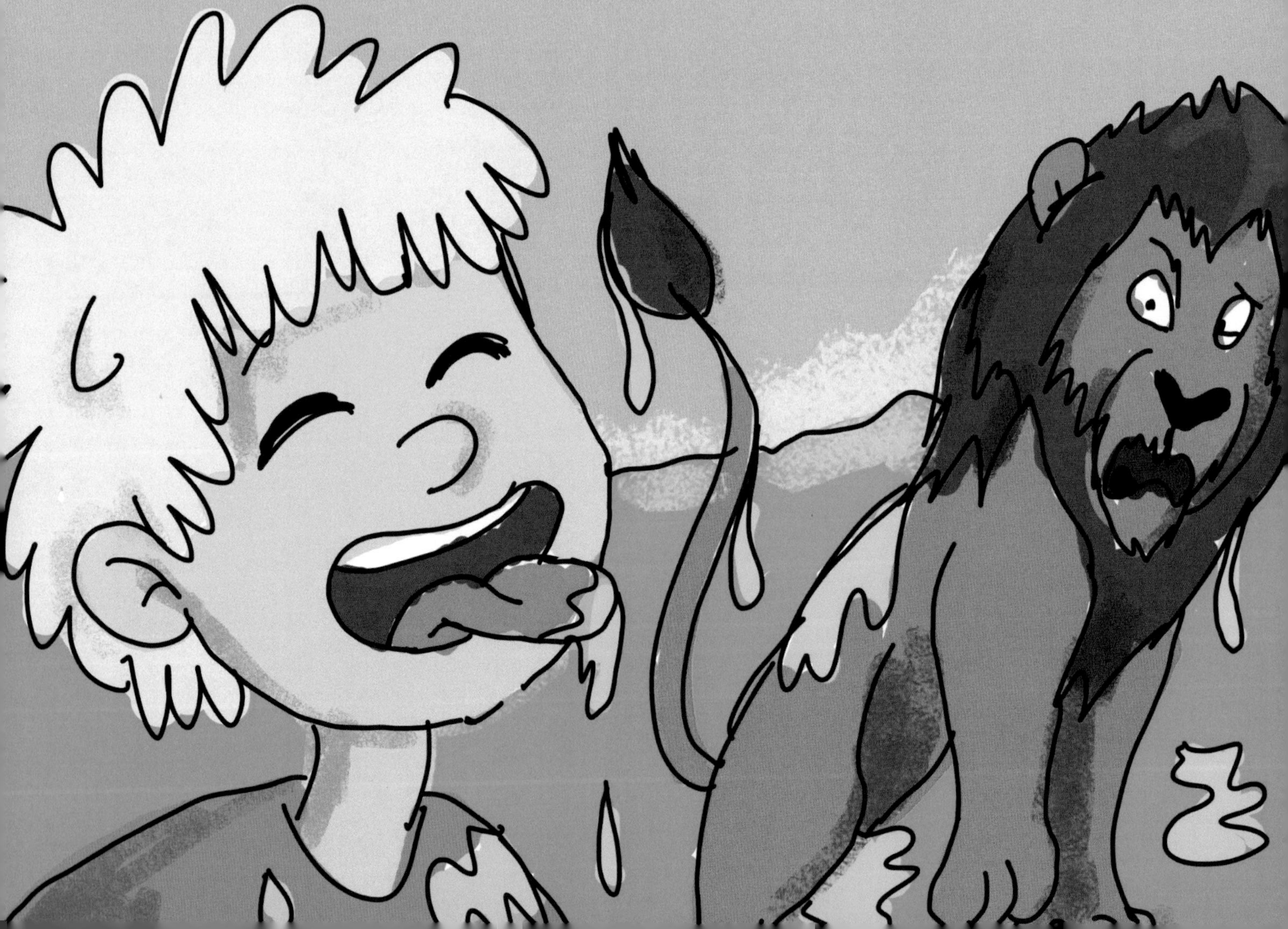

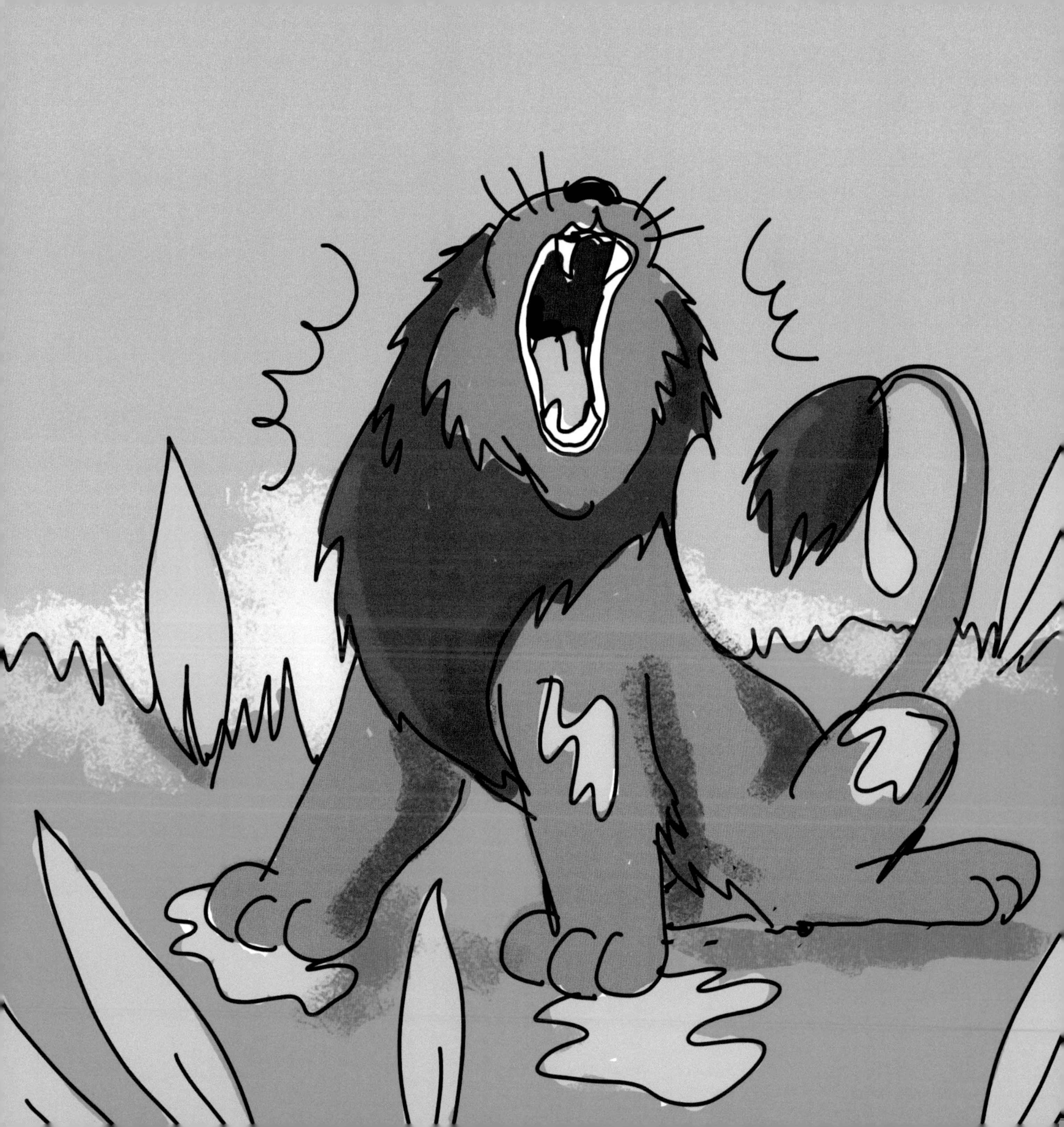

But, if you still decide to do it,
Then I have a hunch
That you **WILL** get to lick a lion,
And the lion **WILL** get lunch!

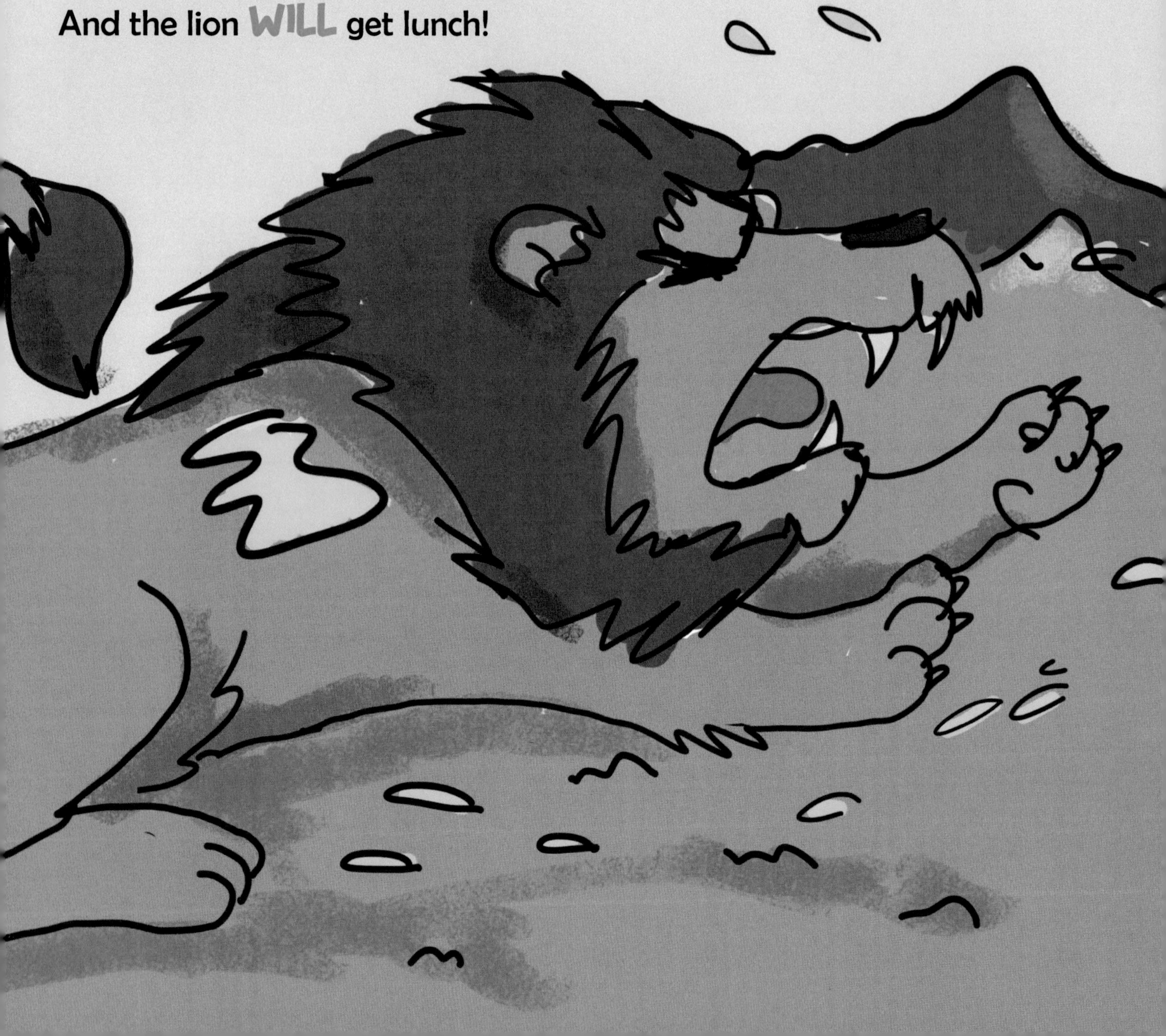

Oh. Don't forget...

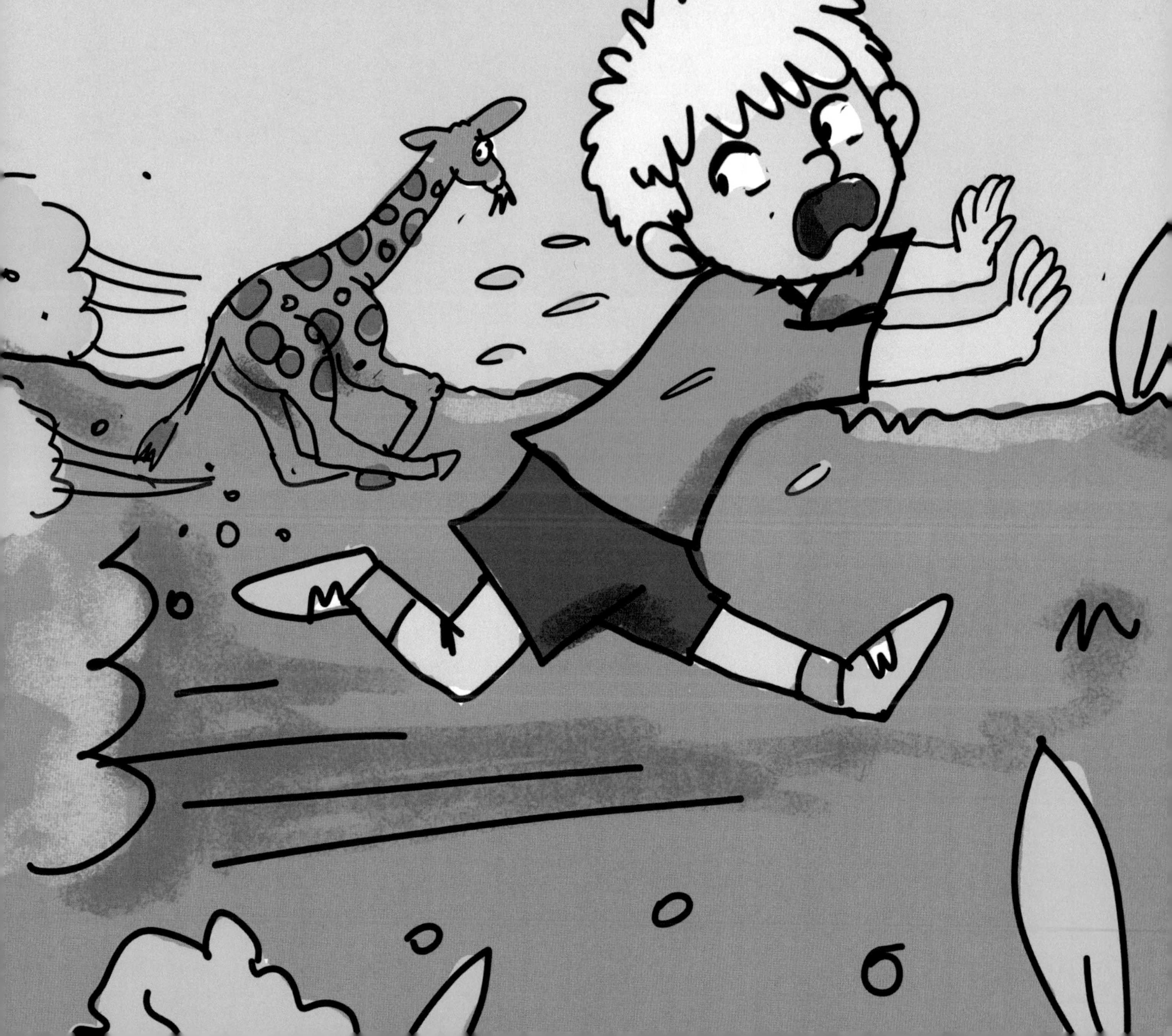

Never EVER lick a lizard,
I'll spare you no expense.
In telling you the reasons why,
I won't keep you in suspense.

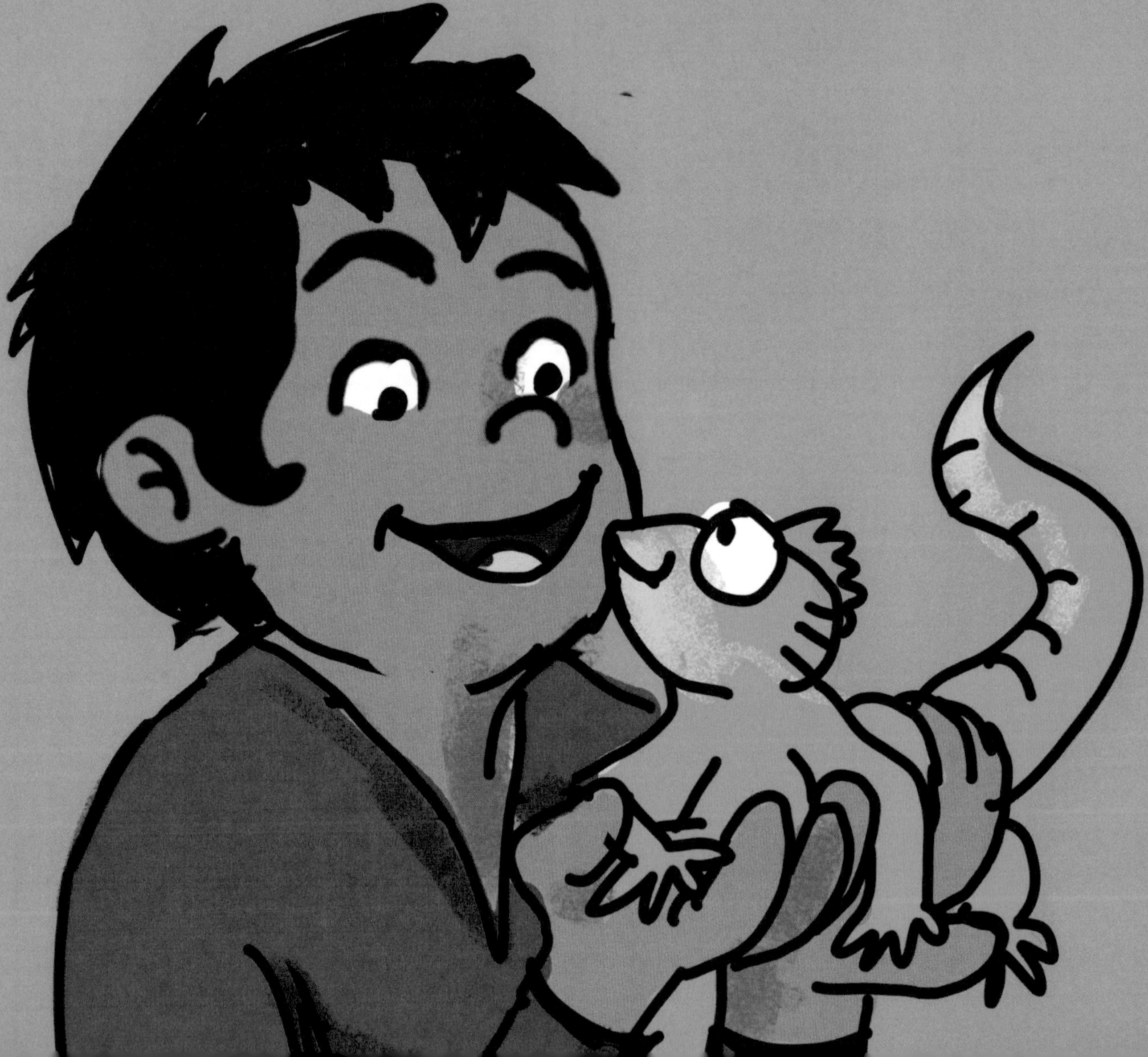

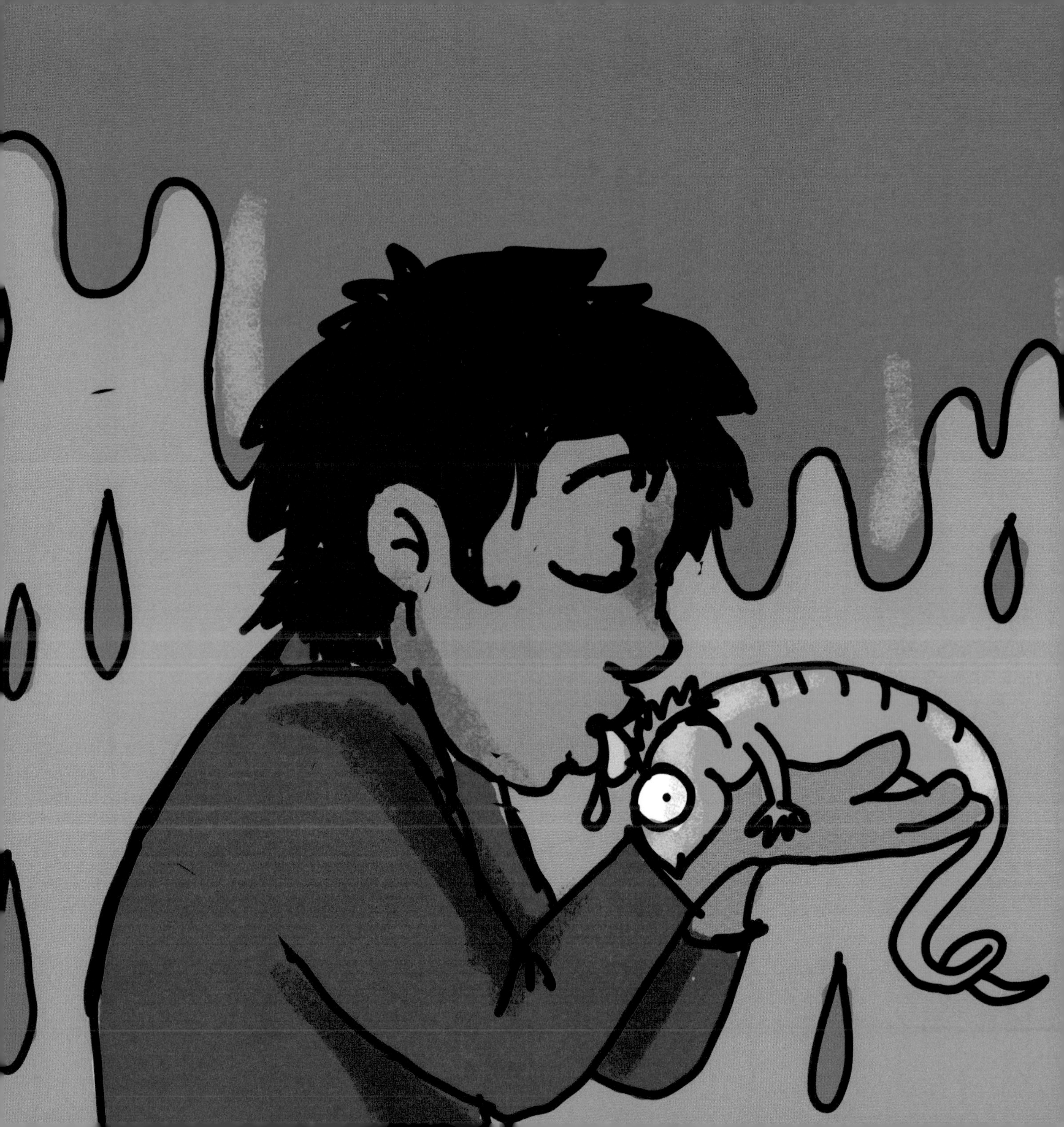

First up, well, lizards have blue tongues.
So if it licks you back,
You'll look like you're the victim
Of a random Smurf attack!

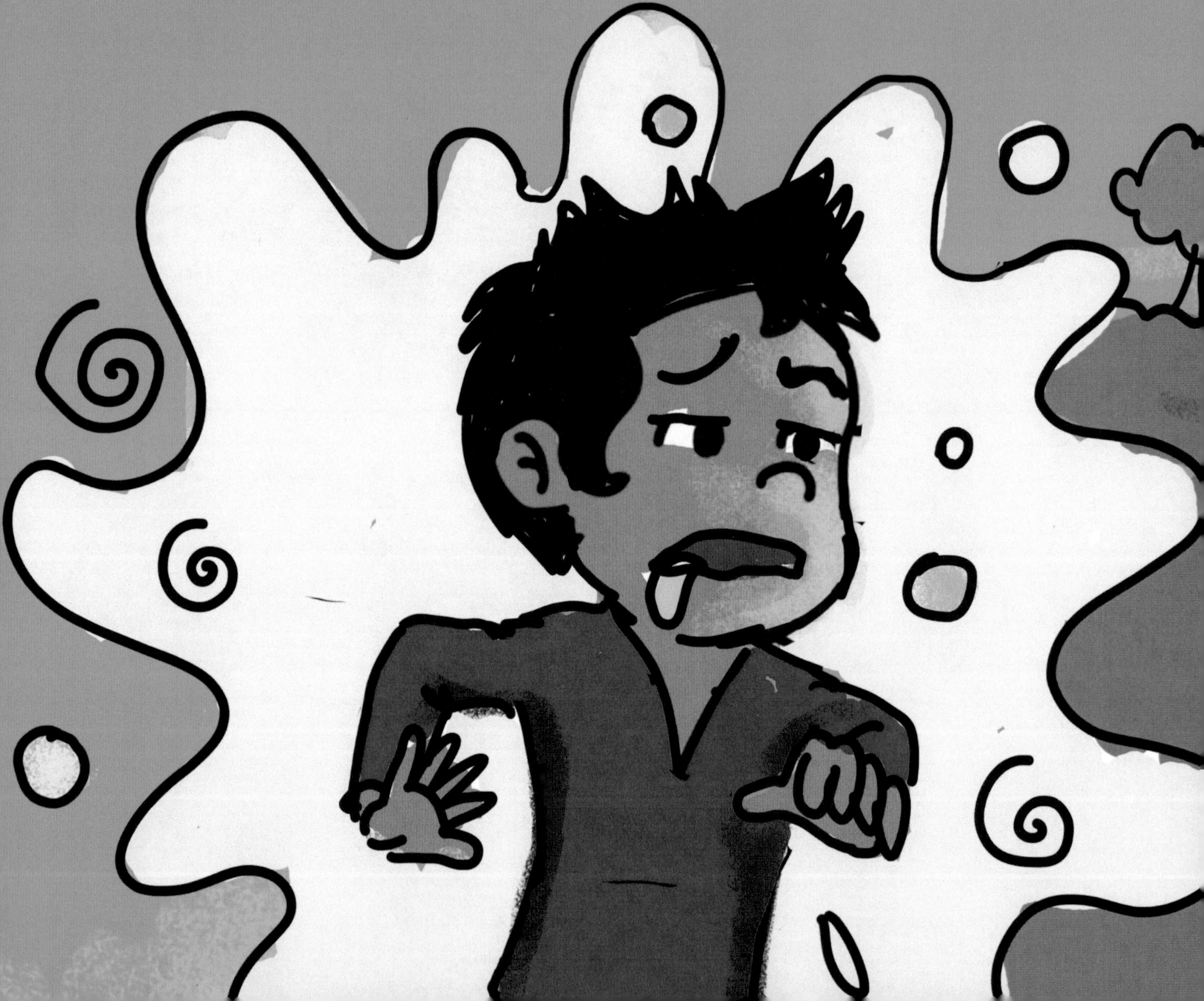

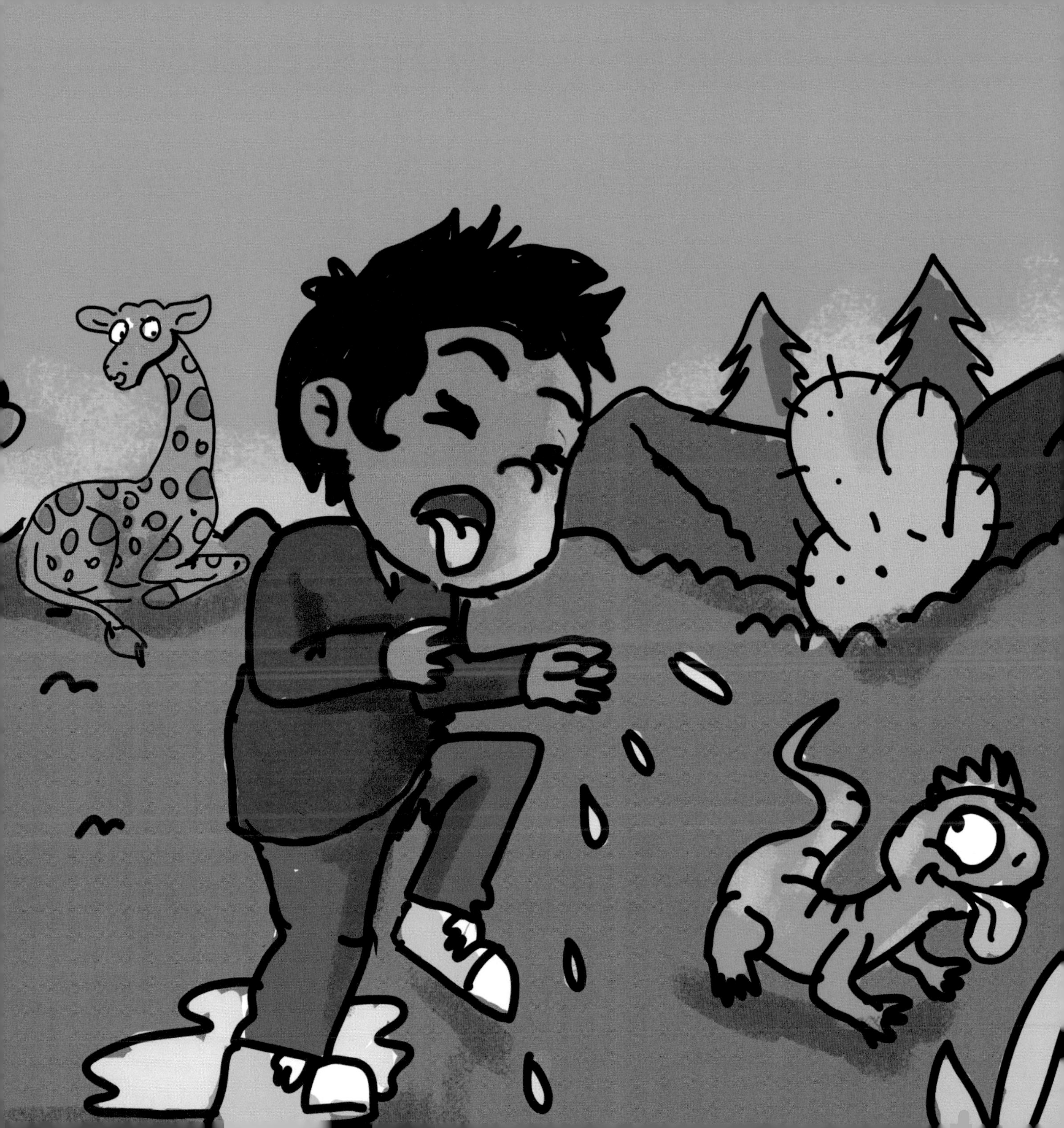

Secondly, a lizard
Looks rather like a snake.
Licking a snake by accident?
That's a mistake you **DON'T** want to make!

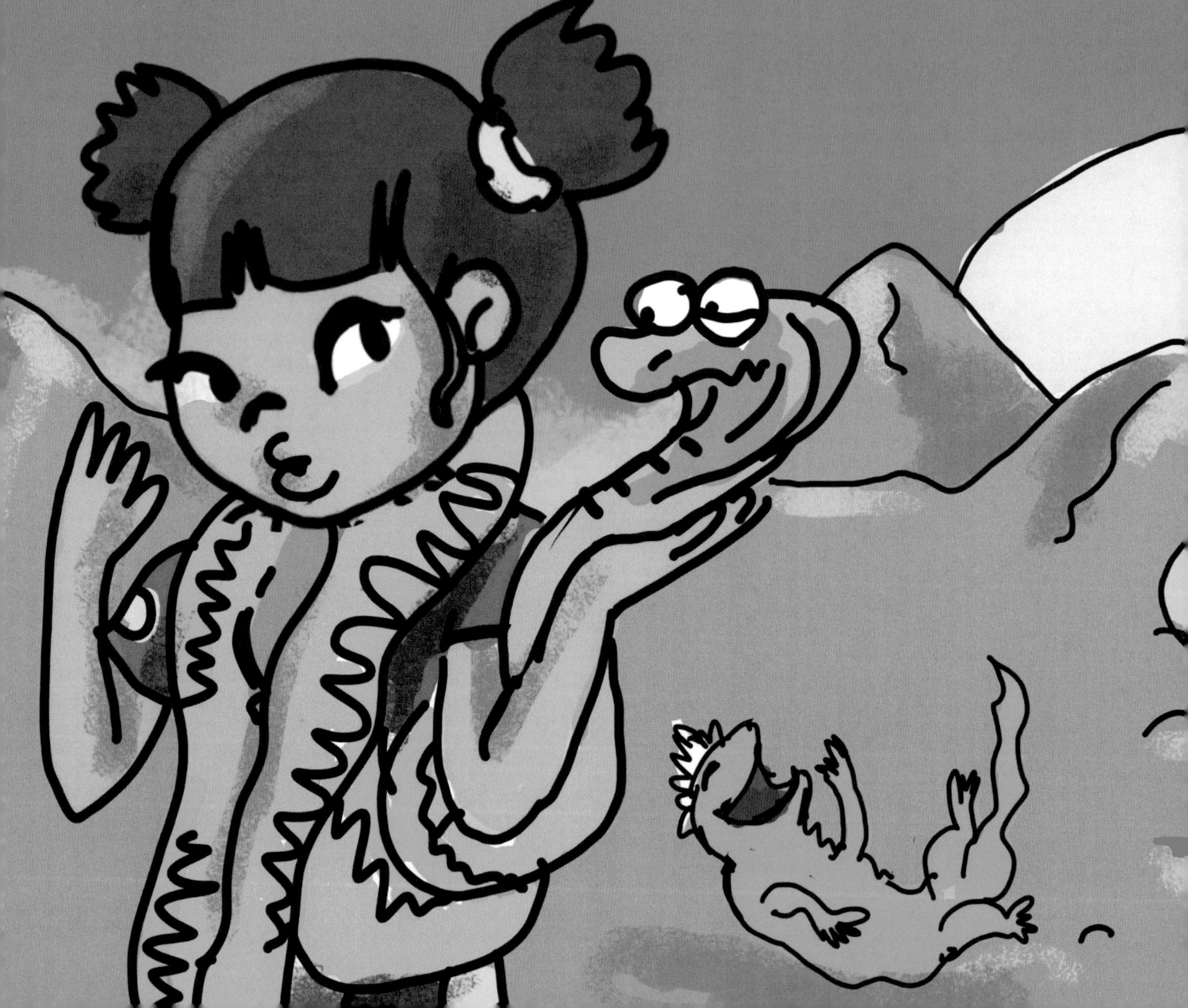

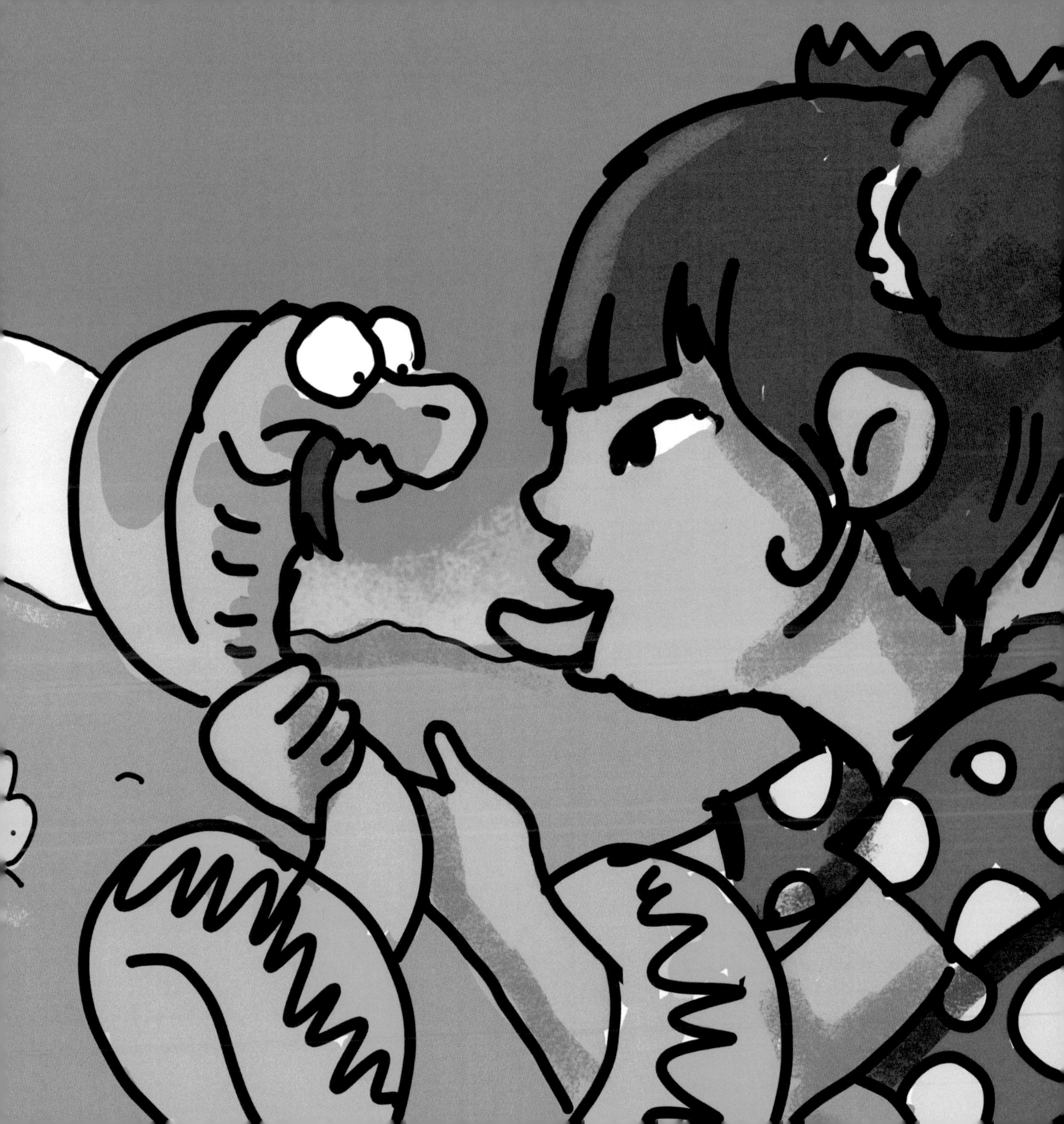

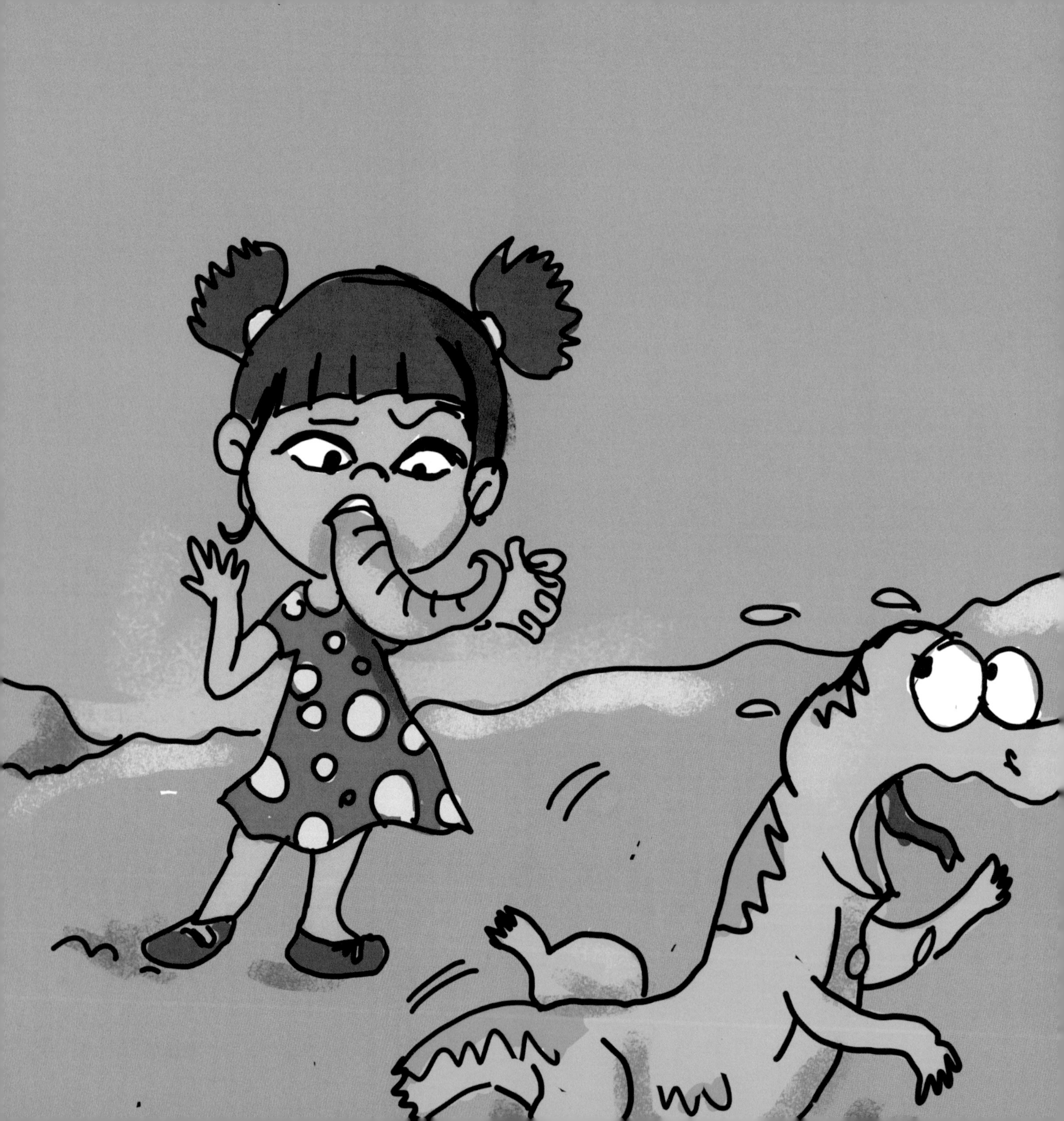

And then, of course, the final reason
Licking lizards is a fail
Is that if it does a drop and run,
You'll get a mouthful of tail!

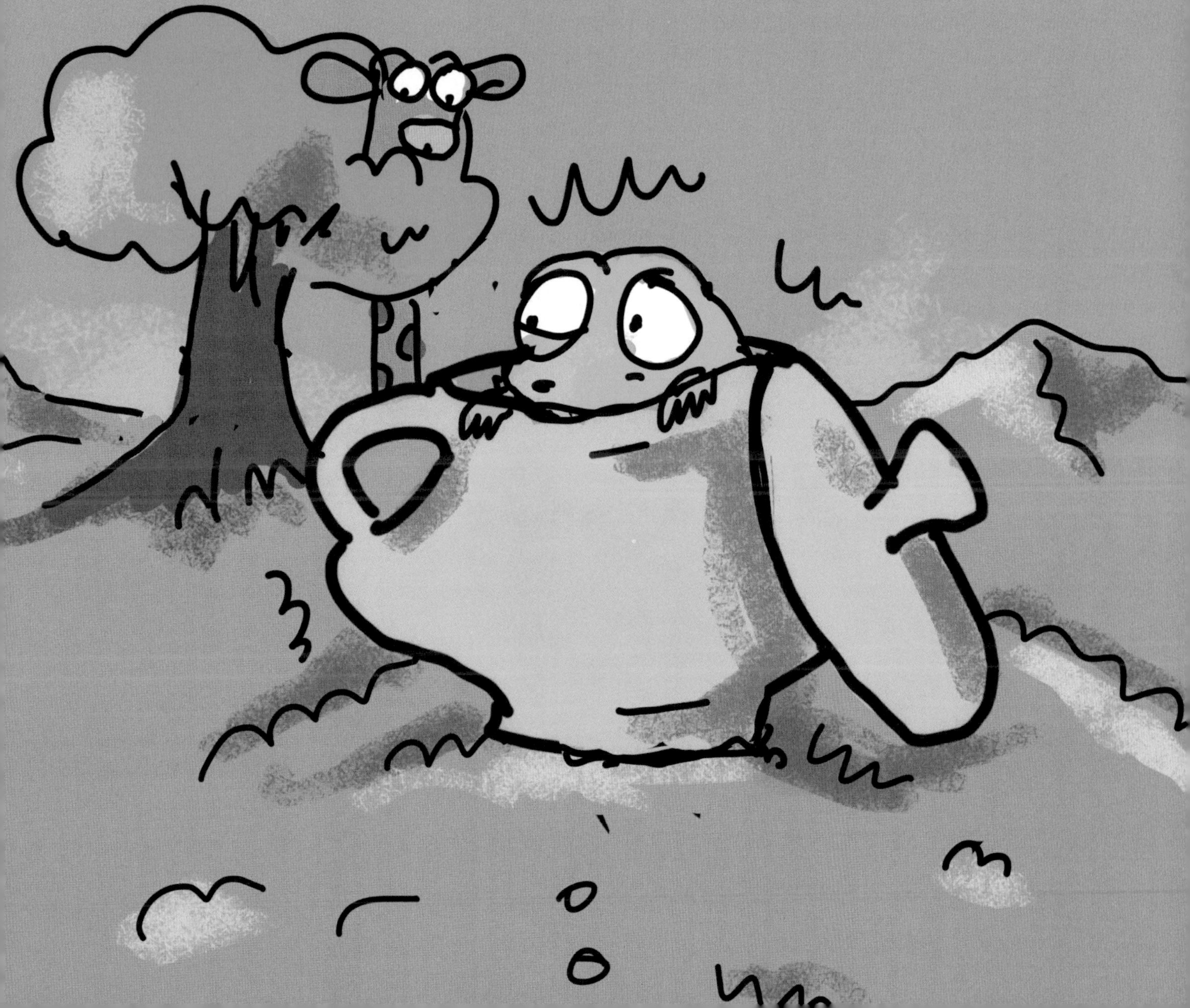

So never **EVER** lick a lizard,
A lion or a llama.
Unless, of course, you want a life
Filled with animal-licking drama!

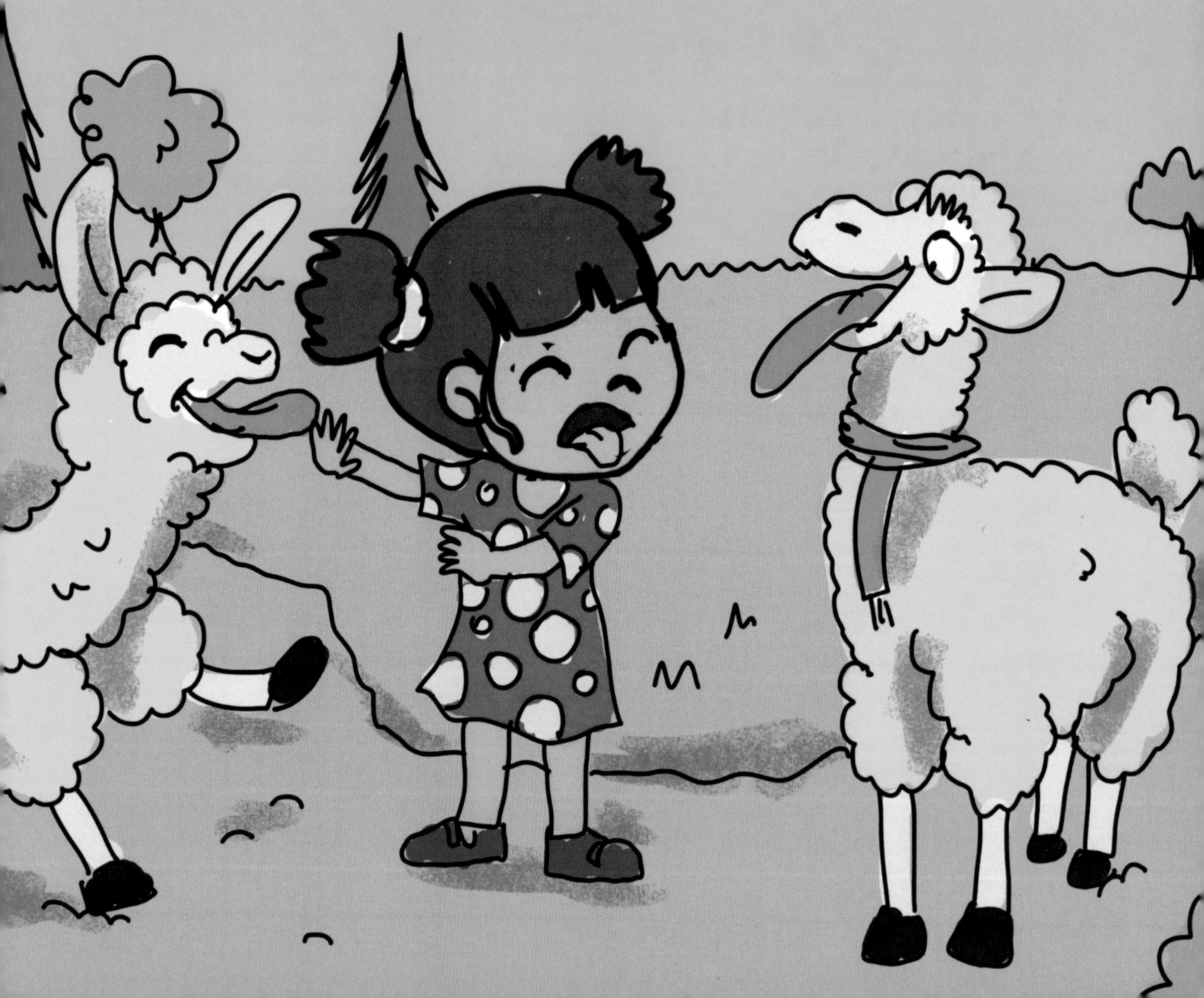

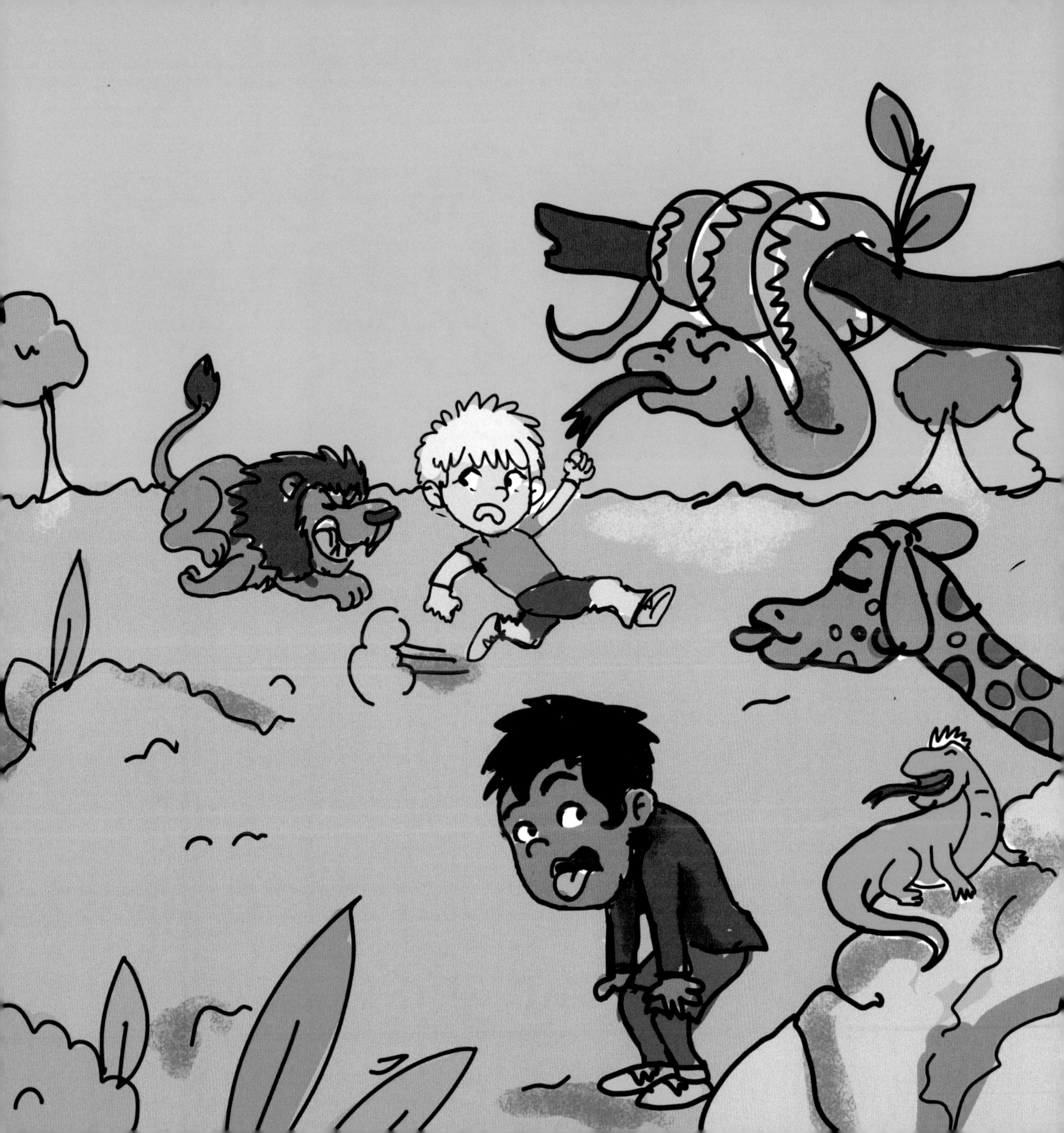

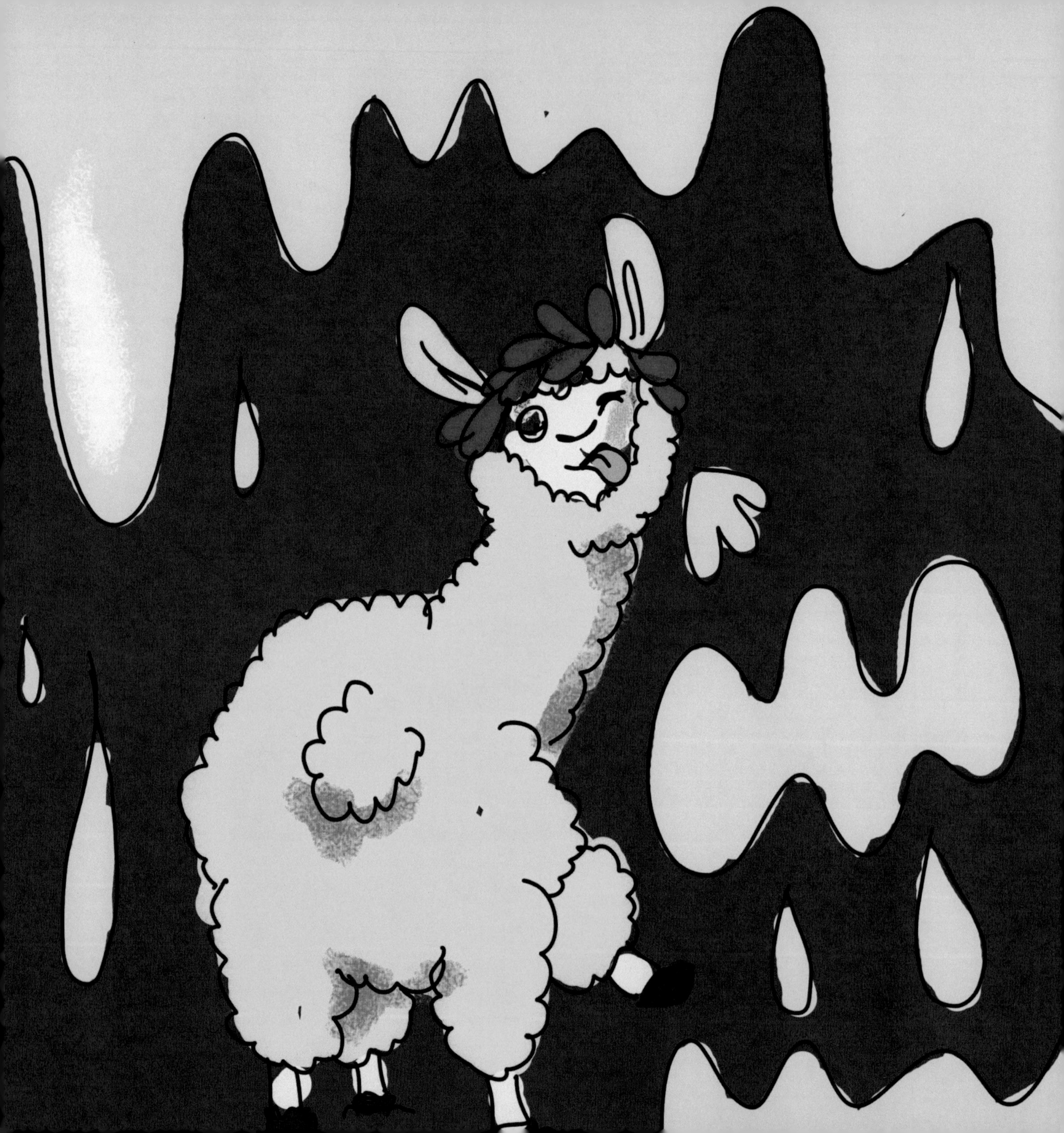

@marynhin

Mary Nhin   Adam Wallace

Grow Grit   Wallace100

NEVEREVERBOOKS.COM

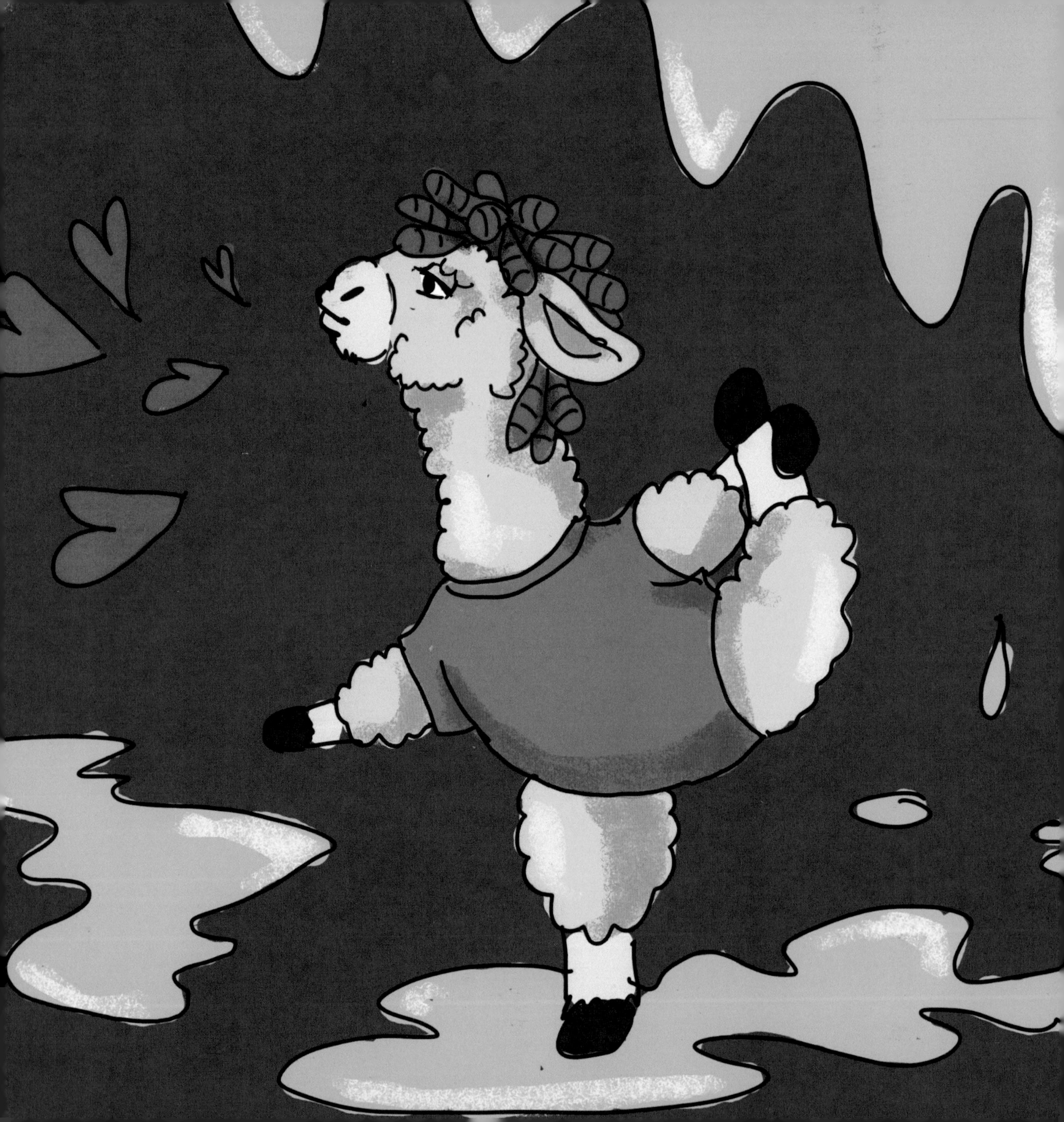

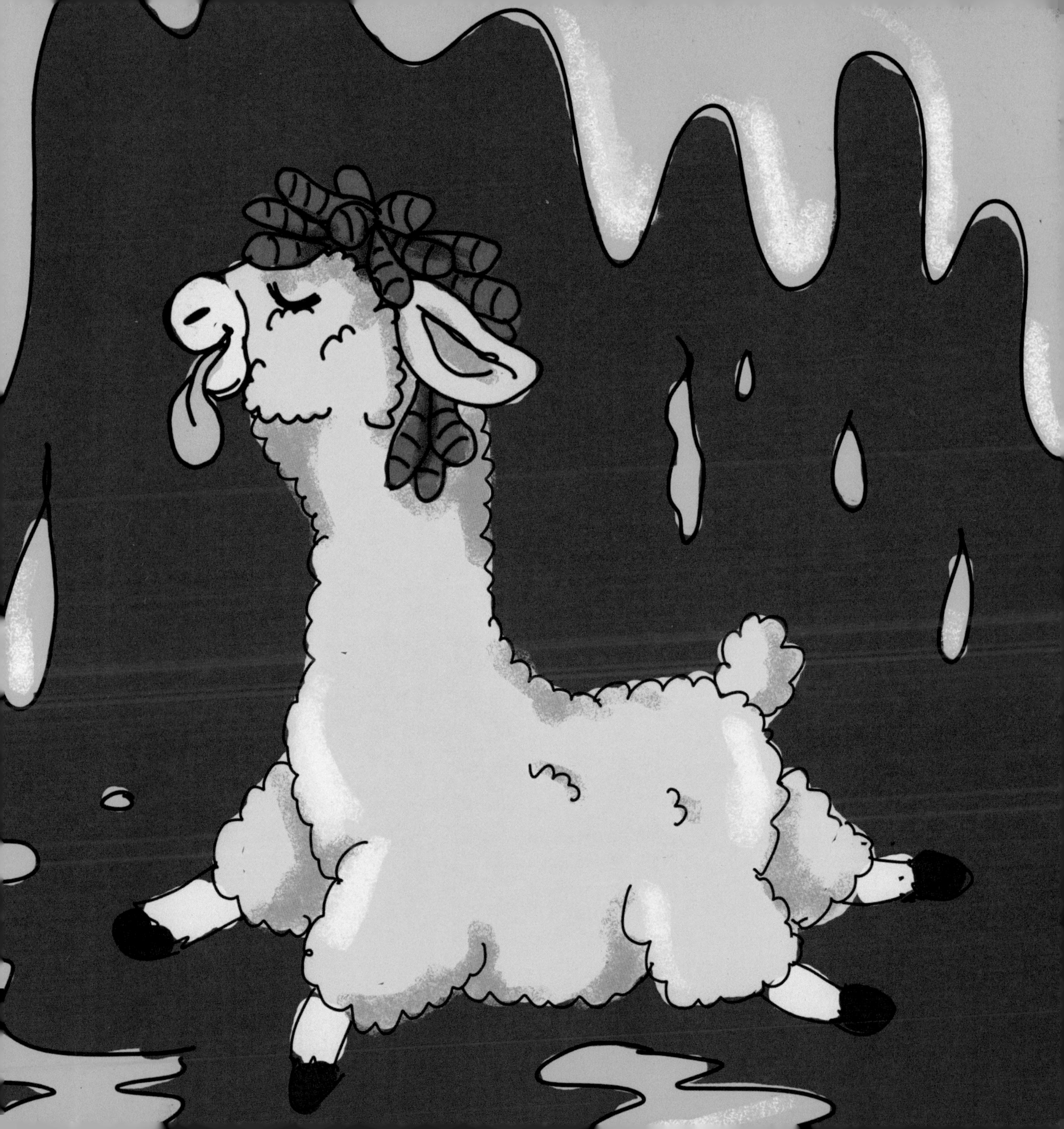

Made in the USA
Coppell, TX
14 October 2023

22817030R10021